"It was a shock!" Jo glared at him

"I was not expecting to be jumped on."

The sardonic smile grew. "More of a shock than diving headfirst into a mountain lake?" Seb sounded intrigued.

"Much," Jo said crushingly.

"I knew it was exceptional," he said in a satisfied tone. Their eyes met, his lazily amused, but somehow quite implacable. "Something happened out there, though. I want to know what it was. One minute you were kissing me—really kissing me—and the next...."

Jo's throat suddenly felt like sandpaper. It was an effort to bring her eyes to his face. "What?"

"You were looking scared to death."

Sophie Weston wrote and illustrated her first book at the age of five. After university she decided on a career in international finance, which was tremendously stimulating and demanding, but it was not enough. Something was missing in her life, and that something turned out to be writing. These days her life is complete. She loves exciting travel and adventures, yet hates to stray too long from her homey cottage in Chelsea, where she writes.

Books by Sophie Weston

GYPSY IN THE NIGHT
Sophie Weston

Harlequin Books

TORONTO • NEW YORK • LONDON
AMSTERDAM • PARIS • SYDNEY • HAMBURG
STOCKHOLM • ATHENS • TOKYO • MILAN

Original hardcover edition published in 1991
by Mills & Boon Limited

ISBN 0-373-03186-6

Harlequin Romance first edition March 1992

GYPSY IN THE NIGHT

CHAPTER ONE

JO PAGE swung her long tanned legs out of the open-topped Mercedes and gave Simon Curtis a sweet smile.

'Thank you,' she said. 'That was—instructive.'

Simon looked faintly alarmed. 'Seb will brief you properly,' he said.

'I'm sure he will.' Jo reached for her single, compact case and hauled it out by its shoulder-strap from the back seat.

'I'm only the messenger,' Simon said hurriedly. 'You don't want to take too much notice of me.'

Jo's green eyes gleamed. It was a look that had made stronger men than Simon Curtis uncomfortable.

'But I always take notice of messengers,' she assured him, straight-faced.

'Oh, lord,' said Simon, harassed.

Laughing, Jo relented. 'You haven't told me anything I didn't expect.'

It did not seem to reassure him. He sat with both hands gripping the borrowed steering-wheel, looking up at her.

'When someone pays me twice my normal fee—and my normal fee is the top of the market—to do a stunt programme that any halfway fit amateur could do...' She shrugged. 'Well, it sets up a few question marks.'

And more than a few alarm bells. Though there was no point in worrying Simon even more by saying that now.

He did not seem entirely reassured. He was staring straight in front of him, brows knit. Jo felt sorry for him. This was his first big job in films and Seb Corbel would not be the easiest director to start off with.

'I won't tell him you were indiscreet,' she promised.

Simon flashed her a quick look at that. 'Kind of you,' he said drily.

It was Jo's turn to look away. She knew as well as Simon evidently did that on that long trip from the airport into the Spanish mountains she had been deliberately drawing confidences out of him.

She had been justified, she felt. She had been uneasy about the job from the start, and everything Simon had said had confirmed her feelings. But that did not disguise the fact that she had set out to manipulate him.

He said slowly, 'You've been very clever.'

Jo hesitated. But the door of the village house opened and a small grey-haired woman in black appeared at it, beaming.

'Pepita,' Simon said. 'This is Miss Page,' he added in slow, careful Spanish. 'Show her the room we discussed, will you?'

And Pepita, nodding and replying at a speed which made nonsense of Simon's laboured communication, seized the strap of Jo's case and urged her away from the car and up an outside staircase.

Jo went, laughing.

'I'll be back later,' Simon shouted after her, putting the great car in gear and setting it moving up the narrow street.

Over her shoulder she called out, 'See you!'

She heard the car's engine in the still air long after it had disappeared between the narrow white-painted houses. Then, shrugging slightly, she followed Pepita.

The white staircase curved round the side of the little house, painted a dazzling white. Under her hand the stone wall was warm. It was clear that she was to be housed on the roof. Sighing a little, Jo hoisted her bag over her shoulder, declining Pepita's offer to take it with a smile.

In the course of her career, she had slept in the simplest of accommodation. But she had hoped that *Dangerous Midnight*, with its big-name director and international cast, would have provided at least a sprung mattress and twentieth-century plumbing.

She wondered where the actors were staying. Not in this simple village, she was sure. Anna Beth Arden would be looking for a four-star international hotel at the very least.

As Jo expected, Pepita showed her to a roof room, half exposed to the open air. Jo looked round. What it lacked in modern comforts it more than made up in charm. The low Arab-style bed was covered with a woven rug. The area itself was half-terrace, half-bedroom. There was a set of pulleys which Pepita demonstrated, to show Jo how to lower the swathed hangings if it was cold or rained. Her whole expression said that it was inconceivable that either might happen.

Jo nodded agreeably and went to the low parapet. The view over the little hill village and out to the mountains was breathtaking. Pepita followed her, pleased with Jo's pleasure.

The terrace was filled with pots of bright geraniums growing out of earth as dry as cement. Jo searched her memory for her last visit to Spain.

'Linda,' she managed at last, indicating her pretty surroundings.

Pepita was pleased by even so simple an attempt to speak her own language. She beamed even more widely and waved her hands, indicating plainly that Jo was to make herself at home. Then, promising iced coffee in an instant, she disappeared down the curved staircase.

Even this high up, it was so hot that the air lay on Jo's skin like a blanket. She took off her cotton blouse and pulled a T-shirt out of her case. Without much hope, she looked for a bathroom.

A shower cabinet in the corner smelt musty and had no discernible pipework. This, she thought ruefully, was going to be an adventure. Jo pulled on her T-shirt and sank gratefully into one of the painted basketwork chairs on her terrace.

She tipped her head back and closed her eyes. The air was warm against her eyelids. Deliberately she let herself relax.

She sat without moving, grateful for the peaceful heat. Without identifying them, she was conscious of the foreign scents that wafted up to her. Somewhere below, a car arrived. There was a splutter of Spanish. A door slammed. Jo dreamed on, unmoving.

She did not hear anyone come up those stairs, though they echoed like a medieval prison. She did not sense any movement. But suddenly she knew she was no longer alone.

Startled, her eyes flew open. She turned her head, half expecting to see Simon's worried figure. She was already smiling.

Only it was not Simon standing at the top of the stairs considering her. It was no one she had ever met.

He was a tall man, broad-shouldered and long-legged. Jo stared at him, still dazed, seeing the still figure like some devil that had materialised out of a wall painting: thin as whipcord with the tough face of a fallen angel. There were grey slashes across the black hair at his temples. Meeting cynical brown eyes, Jo's instinctive smile died as if he had thrown cold water in her face.

She might not have met him but she knew him all right. There had been too many photographs for her not to. Though he did not look like his photographs, she thought, struggling to clear her head. He looked darker and more dangerous than the laid-back personality the interviewers talked about. Seb Corbel did not seem pleased.

Jo came to her feet and lifted her chin a fraction. He seemed not to notice.

'Jo Page?' The voice was much more what she might have expected if she had thought about it: low and slightly husky. It was a very attractive voice and she was almost sure that he knew it. Her eyes narrowed.

He strolled forwards. In spite of that impression of leashed power, he moved with a lazy grace that made him look as if he had never rushed or hustled in his life. At close quarters, Jo had to acknowledge, the personality was overwhelming.

Jo resisted the temptation to put her hands behind her back but, even though she shook his offered hand, she noticed that she gave ground before him and was annoyed by it.

He did not introduce himself. He must know he did not need to. Seb Corbel had had his picture in too many papers, attending too many prize ceremonies this year, for it to be necessary. She tried not to let that annoy her. They were going to be working together, after all. She could not afford to fight with the director.

His eyes flicked over her. The forbidding expression disappeared as if it had never been.

'Good of you to come,' he drawled with an easy, automatic charm that set her teeth on edge.

She ought to have been gracious; it would have cost so little to have murmured a couple of pleasantries about how she was looking forward to working with him. But she was tired and on edge, and his silent appearance had overset her oddly.

'You're paying me,' Jo reminded him tartly.

The diabolical eyebrows flew up, and Jo saw in a split second that he had been thinking exactly the same thing. She bit her lip in vexation.

'Great personal inconvenience, I understood from Jerry. And you turned me down first time round,' he said softly. His eyes were brown and hard as stone. There was speculation in them. 'How did you manage to free yourself up after all? Something fall out of the schedule?'

There was a whole range of answers to that, all of them complicated and none of them particularly flattering to Seb Corbel and his prestigious production. Nor, thought Jo, did she want to have to explain herself to her new employer. It was enough that he knew she had not wanted the job; and that he had had to pay a high price to get her in the end.

Meeting his gaze levelly, Jo decided she did not like him. She did not like the sexy voice or the cold mockery in those eyes.

'I imagine you are well aware of why I agreed to come,' she said evenly.

Seb Corbel's eyes narrowed as if she had surprised him. Good, she thought, on a little kick of triumph. It was childish, but she did not want this man thinking he could read her.

'Money is a great persuader,' he agreed drily.

She tensed but refused to drop her eyes. 'As you say.'

There was a small silence. She thought she had surprised him again and that he did not like it. Tension vibrated between them. Jo found she was standing with her shoulders back and her chin high as if she were in the dock. Seb Corbel's eyes swept up and down and up her body again. She felt shaken as if he had touched her, but all he said was, 'You're taller than Anna Beth.'

Jo said with less than her usual composure, 'I've stunted for her before.'

He nodded. It was obviously no surprise to him. Jo wondered whether he had made the connection between that previous professional relationship and her extreme reluctance to take on this new film.

'What do you think of the screenplay?'

She stared at him. For a wild moment she thought he was asking for literary criticism of his masterpiece. He saw the blank amazement in her face and gave a low laugh.

'I was thinking of the stunts,' he said lazily, answering her unspoken surprise. 'Simon tells me you think an amateur could do them. A "halfway fit amateur", if I recall.'

Quoted back at her, it sounded horribly arrogant. She bit her lip. Damn Simon. The brown eyes mocked her.

'The voice of experience,' murmured Seb Corbel provocatively. 'You can do it?'

Jo drew a long breath, but she bit back the heated retort that sprang to her lips. She had enough sense to realise that the hateful man was baiting her.

'Naturally,' she said, without expression.

He laughed. 'Naturally. You're the best, aren't you?'

Jo shrugged. 'Not necessarily. You had Helena Kapinski to begin with, didn't you? She's a trained gymnast.'

'She was the first one,' he agreed pleasantly. 'When you turned me down.'

Jo flashed him a look of surprise. 'It was hardly that personal.'

'No? And yet I got the impression from your agent that you wouldn't work for me come hell or high water.'

Jo felt her colour rise. But she said steadily, 'You must have misunderstood.'

'Yes?' He sounded sceptical.

'I'm here, aren't I?' she said. 'It was only that I couldn't do it when you wanted.' It was a lie. She did not even know why she bothered to tell it. He clearly did not believe her. 'What happened to Helena?' she asked hurriedly.

Seb's face was unreadable. 'She had an accident.'

Jo stared. Helena was tough, agile and experienced; and careful.

'That's not like her.'

'I was—surprised. I thought professional stunters didn't have accidents,' Seb agreed. The lazy voice sounded weary. 'But she got reckless.' He turned and looked out at the mountains. 'It must be something in the air,' he mused. 'Or the movie's jinxed. Since that, it's been one damn thing after another.'

Jo stiffened. 'On the stunts?'

Seb shrugged. 'Mainly. After Helena we used a local girl. It didn't work out. Then we got Sally Stegmann. *She* seemed to be undergoing some personal crisis.'

He sounded, Jo thought, utterly bored. Her dislike flamed up and she repressed it firmly. Instead she concentrated on what he had told her.

'And after that the agencies couldn't find you any more replacements?' It sounded like a challenge, she realised too late. As if she were saying that the agencies had blacklisted the movie.

But Seb Corbel's eyes crinkled in amusement as he registered the combative note. He took it calmly—as, Jo was beginning to realise, he took everything.

He gave her a slow smile that made her feel as if he had run his fingers up her spine. Jo shivered involuntarily and was furious with herself when she met his bland expression.

'Ah, but they did, didn't they?' Seb said lazily. He strolled over to the parapet and looked out across to the distant skyline again. 'To be honest, the stunts have been appalling. I wasn't going to waste any more time. So I told Jerry to get me the best. At any price. Which you most certainly are—and cost.'

Jo felt her colour rising for the second time. She held on to her poise though.

'I'm flattered,' she said coolly.

But she wasn't.. She was scared.

When Seb's casting director had first approached her, months ago, she had told her agent to turn it down without a second thought.

Jerry had not been particularly concerned. There was plenty of stunt work around and Jo Page had her fair share of it. But he had been surprised.

'Why not? If we juggle a bit, you could fit it in.'

Jo had shrugged. 'I'd rather fit in a holiday. Remember those, Jerry? You take a book and a picnic and lie under a tree somewhere without a phone.'

The agent shuddered, grinning. 'Don't even talk about it. It gives me nightmares. Seriously, why don't you take this? It's in the south of Spain. You could stay on for that holiday afterwards.' He gave her a shrewd look. 'Don't get on with Seb?'

Jo shook her head. 'I've never met the man.'

Jerry said, 'Well, he has a bit of a reputation and I know you don't like that sort of thing...'

It was an old joke. Jerry had seen off more than one importunate suitor who had misread Jo's professional friendliness. He called it riding shotgun, and never ceased to be amused by it when she called on his assistance. Though he never let her down.

Jo laughed. 'You think I'm very prim, don't you, Jerry?'

He gave a bellow of laughter. 'Honey, prim is the last thing I think you are. Hell, anyone who can launch herself out of a helicopter the way you do has gone way beyond vicarage tea-parties. But I know you have standards. Seb Corbel isn't the type to appeal to you.'

She did not comment on his remark about Seb Corbel. They had both read the gossip.

'If I only worked with directors who appealed to me, I'd be on the dole,' Jo said crisply.

Jerry did not deny it. He continued to look at her quizzically, his blue eyes shrewd and not unkind.

Jo hesitated, then said, 'To be honest, Jerry, it's the girl I'd be doing the stuff for.'

The blue eyes widened. Jerry said, 'Ah.' He looked down at the typewritten letter in front of him. 'The Arden girl? Hollywood's white hope?'

'That's the one. Anna Beth Arden.'

'Bit of a baggage, is she?'

Jo said carefully, 'Let's say I would prefer not to work with her again. If it can be avoided gracefully.'

Jerry's eyes narrowed. Jo was calm and professional. She had no temperament to speak of, and she bore the whims of actors and directors alike with good humour while she did her best to fulfil their sometimes lunatic ideas. She certainly did not take unreasonable dislikes to people.

He said slowly, 'Anything I should know?'

Jo hesitated. 'Not without my risking a slander suit. Only—put it this way, Jerry; if you send someone out to stunt for Anna Beth Arden, you'd do well to increase her insurance cover.'

'Ah,' said Jerry again. He looked down at the letter in his hand and scribbled something on the top before flicking it into his 'out' tray. 'I don't think we're going to be able to help Mr Corbel.'

Only now, here she was sitting on a hot, high terrace with Mr Corbel and wishing that she was anywhere else in the world.

If it weren't for the money...

But even the money would not have mattered if her father had been a different man. Or if her grandfather had learned how to save instead of spend money. Or if her stepmother were less of an expensive luxury. Or...

Jo sighed. There was no point in thinking about it. She was in a trap and the money from this film was the only hope of escape.

Seb Corbel said curiously, 'What is it that you don't like about me?'

Jo jumped. She had been so wrapped up in her own thoughts that she had been oblivious to his steady inspection. Now she lifted her head to find the brown eyes squarely on her.

'I don't...' she began, flustered.

But he said, 'Jerry was quite clear.'

'Oh.'

What had Jerry said?

With an amusement not unlike Jerry's own, Seb Corbel said, 'I got the impression that you don't—er—care for my style.'

Thank you, Jerry, Jo thought savagely. But she kept a cool face.

'Would it help,' Seb asked lightly, 'if I undertook to keep my hands off you?'

There was a silence while Jo felt herself freeze into immobility. Then the embarrassment swept through her like a forest fire. She put her hands to her hot face.

'I never... Jerry shouldn't... It wasn't...'

Seb was watching her with interest.

'I can see it wouldn't,' he said thoughtfully. 'Oh, well, I shall have to find some other way to reassure you. I can't afford to have another stunt girl walk out on me, you see,' he explained with a glint in his eye, as Jo's hands fell. 'Otherwise it might be worth it.'

Jo let that pass. She said with difficulty, 'I'm sorry. Jerry—well, he had to talk me into this film and I suppose he was in a bit of a temper. But he shouldn't have said that.'

'In a temper with you?'

'Yes.'

It had not been an easy interview. Seb Corbel had won the Oscar by then, the big one, and Jerry was anxious to do him a favour. The agency was successful but not yet big on the international circuit. So Jerry had stopped listening to Jo Page by then. And Jo herself had had new problems which her agent knew all about. He had used them ruthlessly to persuade her.

'OK,' Seb said at last. 'You're here under duress. Still, as you pointed out, you're here.' The drawl became steely. 'And you'll do your best for me. Or I'll see you never work on a major picture again.'

That was all she needed, thought Jo. An agent who told tales on her and a director who bullied her with the threat of unemployment.

She said steadily, 'I always do my best.'

He looked sceptical again. But all he said was, 'I'll hold you to that.'

And then Pepita came with a tray of iced coffee, and after a quick exchange of explosive Spanish—which made him suddenly much less lazy—he flickered his fingers at Jo and left her to her drink.

She sipped her coffee and then stretched out on the bed for a while. The encounter with Seb had done nothing for her tiredness or the incipient migraine Jo was afraid she was incubating. She had been jetting round the world rather too much in the last few months, she thought ruefully.

Six months ago she would have given as good as she got, and enjoyed it. Six months ago she would not have let Seb Corbel make her blush like a schoolgirl; or taken his insults in silence. After all, she was as much a professional as he was. She had been stunting for the best part of ten years now, and she was in demand. He could tease as much as he liked, but she probably *was* the best in the world at some of the things he wanted her to do in this film.

Oh, well, it could not take long. Maybe a week or ten days and then she could go back to Glebe Farm and see Grandpa and sleep and sleep and...

There was a clattering sound like someone kicking a wall down. Jo came awake with a jerk, propping herself up on her elbow just in time to see Simon Curtis's head appear at the top of the stairs.

'Oh, good, you're here,' he said in evident relief. 'When you didn't answer I was afraid...' He stopped and drew breath. 'Boobed again, I thought. Seb would have *killed* me. I'm not in his good books today.'

Jo sat up properly and ran her hand through her short dark hair. 'Why not?'

'I've messed everything up. I should have been out with the units and had a car meet you at the airport. And I shouldn't have put you here. Though...' He broke off, biting his lip.

Jo looked round. 'Why on earth not?'

'Too primitive. Doesn't look as if we value you enough.'

She could almost hear Seb saying it. She winced. But she said steadily, 'It doesn't matter. And it will be lovely to sleep out under the stars.'

Simon looked genuinely bewildered. 'What?'

She gestured at the arrangement of pulleys on the far wall. 'The tent is only for when it rains,' she said. 'Which it isn't going to do for several months.'

Simon was impressed. 'You've seen this sort of arrangement before, then?'

'I've slept on roofs and gone without running water before,' Jo agreed. She gave him her sudden, mischievous grin. 'After all, I'm paid to be a tough guy.'

Simon went faintly pink. 'You don't look...' he began and then stopped himself.

But Jo was startled by the spontaneous comment and her clear skin coloured. Her eyes fell away from his and she half turned, so that he could only see her profile.

'I'm sorry,' Simon said. 'Breach of second cardinal rule of the day.'

Jo was surprised out of her brief confusion. He gave a lop-sided smile at her bewilderment.

'Cardinal rule two: never comment on the appearance of lady members of the cast and crew. Even if they like it, the others don't.'

Jo laughed.

'Cardinal rule one: make sure the plumbing works. Or that there *is* any plumbing.' He looked at the decayed shower cabinet and shook his head. 'Seb only gave me the job because he knows my uncle. If I go on like this, he's going to sack me before I've finished my first movie with him.'

He sounded very young, although Jo thought he could not be much less than her own twenty-six years. But then, she had been on her own for ten years, and it did not sound as if Simon Curtis was wholly out of the family nest, even now.

'I won't complain,' she promised.

He was rueful. 'It's too late. He said I was to take you up to the main house. Like now. I mean, he seemed to think it was quite funny but—well, he can be... Anyway, I mean Seb would be furious if I don't look after you properly from now on.'

Jo laughed and stretched. The T-shirt slipped off her shoulder. In the late afternoon the heat lay on her skin like the touch of a lover.

'So look after me,' she said, waving a hand at the coffee tray.

Simon laughed too and went to pour the last of Pepita's offering into her empty cup.

Behind them a cool voice said on a note of lazy enquiry, 'Do either of you ever intend to get down to any work?'

Jo gasped and twisted round on the couch. The movement dragged the T-shirt down even further. She saw the brown eyes consider her tanned, naked shoulder for a dispassionate moment. Then he turned that lethal gaze on Simon.

But Simon was unmoved. 'We'll go as soon as Jo's ready,' he promised sunnily, handing Jo the cold coffee.

She gulped it down, hauling the T-shirt back into place one-handed, feeling as if she had been flayed by that indifferent gaze.

Simon was obviously not good at reading his employer's moods. Seb sounded mild enough, but underneath Jo could hear that he was exasperated.

'You haven't even loaded her luggage.'

'Oh, she travels light,' Simon said, blithely oblivious of storm signals.

Jo swung her legs round and stood up. Her skirt had ridden high while she had been asleep. He would have seen that too. She wriggled it down and smoothed it over her hips, not looking at either of them.

'One case,' she said.

Seb frowned quickly. His frown turned to blank disbelief when he saw the bag in the corner. 'What the hell...?' he drawled ominously.

'One case,' repeated Jo sweetly. 'That's all I need.'

There was a pregnant silence. Even Simon picked up the vibrations. He looked at Seb in quick surprise.

Unhurriedly, Jo stood up. Seb barred her way.

'Look, sweetheart,' he said between his teeth, 'I know you didn't want to come. I know you're doing us a tremendous favour by taking the job at all. I'm on my knees kissing your shoes even as we speak. But I'm paying you a blasted fortune for the privilege, as you very well know. So you needn't think you can spin on your axis for a couple of days and then push off to your next glamorous photo-call. I've paid an extortionate price for as much of your valuable time as I need, and you're bloody well going to come through.'

Behind them Simon gasped.

Under the hail of words, Jo stood very still. She was used to temper. She had had ferocious abuse hurled at her head for years as a child, and she always dealt with it in the same way: stand still and never speak without thinking. When you do, answer anything you have been accused of clearly and precisely. And don't raise your voice.

Breaking all her own rules, she said fiercely, 'Don't you shout at me, you bully. I have enough in that suitcase to get me through a month—or a year if it has to. I know what I've contracted to do and I'll do it. And you're right. I didn't want the job. I want it even less now. And if you shout at me again I'll *double* the bill.'

His eyebrows flew up. He had strange, strongly marked eyebrows that winged up towards his temple in a fierce curve. It made him look like some barbarian warlord, Jo decided as she broke off, glaring at him. In her fury she had forgotten that she was on rather weak ground with this man. As the fury seeped away she remembered it; and swallowed rather loudly.

Then—utterly disconcerting her—the brown eyes gleamed.

'If you try it, I'll sue,' Seb Corbel said with relish. He did not make any attempt to disguise his amusement.

'I'm sure you would,' Jo said coldly.

The damned T-shirt was slipping again. His eyes followed it. They weren't indifferent this time. They were amused. Angrily she hauled the cloth back into place and put on her discarded muslin shirt for good measure. Seb's eyebrows rose wickedly.

Jo closed her case and picked it up. 'I, however, prefer to behave in a professional and temperate manner, unless unendurably provoked.'

It sounded impossibly stuffy as soon as she said it. She really couldn't blame him when the horrible man gave a choke of laughter.

'*Temperate?*' he echoed. 'By golly, I'm glad I haven't seen you when you've got your gander up, then.'

His temper seemed completely restored. He took the case from her.

'Come on, then. Let's go and install you in something worthy of your station—or at least,' he added with a wicked gleam, 'your extortionate salary.'

Simon said plaintively, 'I thought I was supposed to do that.'

'I'm not sure you're up to it,' Seb told him, laughing. 'I don't want to have to pay you danger money as well.'

Well, thought Jo, looking round; she had wondered where the actors were staying, and now she knew. The company had rented a huge hacienda, built round a courtyard of lemon trees and jasmine in a gentle fold of the hills behind Santa Ana. It was obviously a treasured family home—some of the furniture was priceless—but there were books and even toys in the cupboards, as if the people who really lived there had just gone away on a visit and would be back at any moment.

'How long have you been here?' Jo asked over dinner.

She was seated next to Miguel Ramirez, a sound-recording engineer, with Simon on her other side. They were eating at a long refectory table in the courtyard. Seb Corbel was sitting at the far end on the other side of the table next to Anna Beth Arden and Bill Hamilton, the male lead.

Miguel grimaced. 'Six weeks.'

'Six weeks!' Jo was taken aback. 'You were lucky to get this place for all that time.'

Miguel smiled. 'No luck. This is the house where the story is set. Seb said he would only do the movie if he could borrow the house. Andres is an old friend so——' he shrugged '—he took his family to the States until Seb tells him he can have his home again.'

'You mean you've actually been filming here?'

Miguel was surprised. 'Of course. In the library. And the carriage drive. Historical authenticity.'

Jo shook her head. She did not like to say that she had skimmed through the script looking entirely at her own activities. The story, whatever it was, had passed her by.

Simon said now, 'We were supposed to be seven weeks. The overruns are *horrendous*.'

'How many of them have been because the stunts have gone wrong?' Jo asked casually. She made a great business of mopping up the olive oil from her hors-d'oeuvre with some of the crusty bread that had been left in chunks on the table.

Miguel and Simon looked at each other. Simon sighed.

'Not all,' he admitted. 'We've got some high-class temperament here.'

Jo looked up quickly. 'Corbel?'

Both men looked almost shocked.

'Not Seb,' Miguel said positively. 'He's so laid back it's not true.'

Jo thought of the fury she had encountered on the roof-top, and decided that Miguel's English must be less fluent than it seemed. She was about to correct him when Simon astounded her into silence.

'He can be infuriating, old Seb, when he has one of his fits of absent-mindedness. But he doesn't get into huffs about nothing. And one way or another he does what he says he is going to do.'

From which Jo inferred that some of the crew members didn't.

Miguel shrugged again. 'Oh, well, *actors*.'

Simon said positively, 'I've never heard of actors be-having like this. It's been like a kindergarten. Thank goodness they've all gone. Well, apart from Anna Beth and Bill.'

'It's because they're all big names in their own country,' Miguel said kindly. 'This lot are all bankable—and all want to prove they're more important to the film than the others. Hence the tantrums.' He thought for a moment. 'And the American girl doesn't help.'

Simon looked unhappy. 'Anna Beth is very talented...'

The expression on Miguel's face was easy to read. He looked amused and a little sorry for Simon. But Simon was oblivious.

'She's had a bad time with the Press. She's been resting, you know, and when she started this picture they wouldn't let her alone, wanting to know where she'd been; who she'd been with.'

'Wanting to know whether she'd been with Seb,' Miguel murmured cynically.

Simon looked revolted. 'That's nonsense. He wouldn't. Anyway, he's years older than she is.'

Miguel looked at him. For some reason Simon flushed. It made him look even younger.

'They're friends,' he said, so loudly that people further down the table looked up.

Miguel gave another of his shrugs, looking round for the basket of bread. Simon pushed his chair back with a crash.

'I've got a lot to do before tomorrow,' he said stiffly. 'I'll go and get on.'

Miguel watched him go, pulling at a piece of bread in his hands, not eating it. Jo watched curiously.

Eventually he gave a sigh and said, 'Do you know Simon well?'

'I've met him before,' she agreed, 'on a television production.'

'I've never worked with him before.' Miguel sounded worried. 'He seems very—impressionable.'

Jo hesitated. All her instincts screamed at her not to get involved. But Miguel was not noticing her reluctance.

'The girl's bad news. Very beautiful, of course. Very sexy. I don't blame Seb. We've had the photojournalists all over us, and it's great for the picture. But...' He looked down the table at the director and his star performer. 'She's dangerous.'

Jo followed his eyes. Anna Beth Arden was happy. You could see it in the beautiful face, in every relaxed line of the perfect body. She was laughing, the provocative mouth slightly open, her mane of auburn curls dancing as she shook her head at something which had been said to her. She was vibrantly alive. And, Jo could see, compulsively attractive.

She said carefully, 'She's beautiful and talented and on top. But dangerous?'

Miguel looked down at the shredded bread in front of him on the polished table. 'She's like a child. A child who doesn't know right from wrong. And she's just tasting power.'

Jo felt that little chill again. She knew, only too well, what she thought Anna Beth Arden might be capable of. Here was this neutral Spaniard, who had never stunted for the girl, sounding as if he was confirming it.

One of the Spanish girls who was waiting on them leaned over with a flashing smile, and put a huge bowl of fruit in the middle of the table. Miguel said something to her, and she laughed as she went down the table with other bowls.

He offered Jo the bowl. She took a nectarine thoughtfully. He turned away, offering it to his other neighbours.

Miguel turned back to her. 'If you're a friend of Simon's, you'd better brace yourself. He's got it badly and Anna Beth is not very—restrained.'

'He'll need a shoulder to cry on?'

It sounded flippant, which Jo had not really meant it to, and she did not blame Miguel for his impatient look.

'He could need a good deal more than that. She's married, you know. To a powerful man.'

Down the table Anna Beth was leaning against Seb's shoulder, her bright hair spilling over the dark cloth of his shirt. Miguel followed Jo's eyes.

'It doesn't matter to Seb. He's powerful too. And right now he can't do any wrong with the studios.'

'But Simon's a different proposition?' This time she did not sound flippant. In fact, Jo noticed, she sounded concerned. She bit her lip. She did not want to be concerned.

Don't get involved, she reminded herself.

Miguel hesitated. Then he said harshly, 'Simon's in love.'

Jo digested that. She looked down the table again at the glowing girl and the man.

'And Seb Corbel isn't?' she asked cynically.

He gave a snort of laughter. 'Seb can take care of himself,' he said obliquely.

Jo sighed. 'Poor Simon. But perhaps he'll grow out of it.'

Miguel nodded. 'People do. Eventually. Given the chance.'

Jo shifted on her seat and bit into her nectarine. This was uncertain ground. She did not want to find herself exchanging confidences with Miguel or anyone else. And he seemed to be moving in that direction.

'I suppose so,' she said vaguely.

They were all supposed to help themselves to cheese and the salads that stood on a table at the far end of the courtyard. To get there one had to pass the little group at the head of the table. Jo did so, nodding to Seb when he caught her eye as she passed. Anna Beth watched her, not raising her head from his shoulder.

Jo put dressed lettuce on her plate and returned to her seat. Seb had gone. Jo quashed her prejudices and said a polite 'hello' to Anna Beth as she passed her.

The look she encountered surprised her. The melting brown eyes were narrowed to slits and the voluptuous mouth that the journalists raved about was compressed until it nearly disappeared.

'Do I know you?' Anna Beth Arden said in a surprisingly steely voice for a Southern belle.

Jo gave her a level look. 'We worked together in Rhodes,' she reminded her in a neutral tone.

Something flashed in Anna Beth's eyes, as if Jo's reply had disconcerted her. But it was gone at once, and the stony expression disappeared in one of lavish charm.

'Sorry, darling. My memory! Er—make-up?' Her eyes were on Jo's face, innocent of cosmetics, and her tone was sweetly poisonous.

The man sitting next to her shifted in embarrassment. 'Surely you know Jo Page?' he said quickly.

Jo knew Bill for a rather good classical actor, given to doing bit-parts in movies between the London theatre seasons. This was his first starring role. They had worked on the same film before, although they were hardly close friends.

'Gracious,' said Anna Beth in a slow insulting drawl. 'The legendary Jo Page. Seb *is* spoiling me.'

Bill Hamilton winced. Jo stood still for a moment, looking down at the artistically tumbled auburn hair.

Then she said softly, 'He surely is,' in a drawl to match Anna Beth's own. And strolled away.

She was aware of the silence behind her. She was aware too that she had probably not been sensible. She could feel Anna Beth's hostility smouldering after her in waves.

She went back to Miguel and ate her salad quickly, running an eye down the typed running schedule that had been left in her room.

'Do you always eat together like this?' she asked, when she had turned the last page.

Miguel turned back to her easily. 'Yes. If you've got to be here next day, it's not really practical to go further.'

She was disappointed, but not really surprised. 'I'd hoped to see a bit of the country. Maybe even get up to Seville.'

He looked at her approvingly. 'We're on seven-day-a-week call at the moment. Seb is desperate to get it in the can. But afterwards, perhaps I could show you Sevilla. My mother's family come from there. It is a wonderful old city.'

Jo was surprised and pleased. She thought she had been collecting some bad marks from Miguel for her lack of reaction to Simon's plight. She gave him her shy smile.

'I'd like that. Thank you.'

'Miguel offering to show you his tape recorder?' said an acid voice that she knew.

They both turned on their chairs, Miguel grinning. Suddenly Jo wasn't hungry any more. She pushed away the half-eaten salad.

Seb stood there, bracing himself with a hand on the back of each of their chairs, brown eyes glinting wickedly. Jo stiffened.

Miguel said calmly, 'Just a helping hand to a new arrival.' Jo could sense his surprise at her reaction to Seb, though.

Seb drawled, 'You're an opportunist, Miguel. And now the opportunity's over. The lady is mine.'

Miguel shook his head, not misunderstanding. 'You're a slave-driver. What on earth are you going to make the poor girl do tonight?'

Seb said soothingly, 'Only talk to Lisa about costume fittings, and have a quick shuffle through the shooting schedules.'

Miguel turned to Jo. 'He says "quick". Be firm with him. Walk away after an hour.'

She stood up, laughing. 'I turn into a pumpkin at midnight anyway,' she assured him.

Seb politely pulled her chair back for her. She acknowledged it without quite meeting his eyes. Miguel stood up too and gave her a little bow.

'I'll see you tomorrow.'

Seb led the way out of the courtyard, away from the chatter and the lights into the house itself. It was dark, but not really cool. It seemed as if all the dusty heat of the day had been trapped in its dark corners.

He said politely, 'I'm glad you're settling in. How's the room?'

The room, as he well knew, was magnificent. Jo knew quite well that, if so many of the actors had not left, she would not have been housed half as glamorously. She also had a tiny suspicion that the luxury was a sort of teasing comment on the inflated fee Jerry had demanded.

So her voice was stiff when she said, 'Very comfortable, thank you.'

Seb laughed. 'You sound disapproving. Do you have ethical objections to eighteenth-century tapestries *too*?'

So he knew the room, for all his apparent carelessness.

Jo said woodenly, 'It's beautiful.'

He gave a sharp sigh. 'You don't give much, do you, Jo Page?'

She did not understand. In the dark his voice was torn between annoyance and amusement, she thought.

'Ever since you arrived you've been like this. Do you think you could manage to be a bit less grudging? We try to work as a team here, and I could do without the queenliness.'

It was justified. Jo knew it was justified. For some reason it made her furious. Normally she was the most reasonable of people, but for some reason this laughing, lazy man got her on the raw.

She snapped, 'I do what I'm paid for.'

And instantly regretted it.

He swung round on her. In the light which filtered in from the garden he suddenly looked immensely tall. She could feel the anger simmering in him, although when he spoke his voice was mild.

'And what would a friendly word cost?' He lowered over her, seeming to search her face in the shadows. 'A smile, occasionally?'

He took her by the shoulders and she tensed. In a freak flicker of illumination as a car's headlights swept across the far window, Jo saw a look of unholy speculation come into his eyes.

'Even a kiss? I suppose you do kiss?'

The car was gone. A distant hum and then silence was all that remained. The room was suddenly electric.

Slowly—almost reluctantly—Seb Corbel stepped towards her and bent his head. Jo watched him, her feelings in disorder, not quite believing it. It was as if the slash of light of the passing headlights had frozen her to the spot, like some magician's weapon.

His mouth was hard and not very kind. He was a lot angrier than he had allowed himself to appear. But, even allowing for the anger, even allowing for her own outrage, there was a heat in the kiss that stirred Jo unbearably.

It was appalling. She tore herself away from him.

'How dare you?' she spat.

He ran his hand insolently round the curve of her cheek. 'Not very original,' he said. He sounded a little breathless.

'I'm not——' she began.

He flung up his hand. 'Don't tell me. You're not paid to be original.'

The words hurt, for all his light tone. Jo bit her lip and was silenced. He took her arm after a pause and began to lead her through the house again.

'I'm glad to know, though,' he said, almost to himself.

Jo was immediately suspicious. 'Know what?'

He glanced down at her in the half-dark. He was clearly amused.

'That you do kiss, after all.'

CHAPTER TWO

JO CAME awake in a rush. Her heart was thundering so hard that it seemed to shake her bones. She put her hand to her ribs and could feel the muscle shaking.

The man's whisper still seemed to hang in the shadows of the lofty room. Although she knew what it was, Jo struggled up on her elbows and strained to look round the room.

It was the old dream. The same terror, the same helplessness and, waking, the same lingering horror. She put her hands up to her face as she had done earlier to hide that burning blush Seb Corbel had aroused. Her skin was not warm now. It was cold and clammy.

There was nothing untoward in the room. The only movement was her own grey reflection in the dressing-table mirror. The priceless hangings were still. Outside the cicadas thrummed.

The room was still. The door, oak and studded with brass, was firmly closed.

Slowly Jo relaxed. She fell back against the pillows. Her breathing came gradually back to normal. Her heartbeat steadied.

What had brought back the old nightmare? When she first left home, sixteen and precarious, she had thought that the haunting would never leave her. Night after night she had woken up, shaking. Sometimes she would even cry out. Sharing rooms with other girls, on holidays or in rented flats, was an impossibility. When the dream came she was too afraid to go back to sleep. She would make herself a hot drink and sit up, drinking it and reading feverishly, until first light.

That phase had passed, of course. Although the dream never really went away, it came more rarely. She had not had it for months now.

'Damn,' said Jo under her breath.

She must be more run down even than she knew. Or the atmosphere of the film had disturbed her more than she had bargained for. Or Seb Corbel, of course.

She pushed the thought away from her. No man—*no man*—disturbed her to that extent. She turned restlessly on the pillows.

It must be sleeping in an unfamiliar room, Jo told herself firmly. I'm tired too. And the travel is getting me down.

Her more honest self said, Nonsense; you sleep in unfamiliar rooms most of your working life. And how often do you fly intercontinental without calling up old demons?

It couldn't be anything else, Jo said stubbornly.

It *could*, allowed the pitiless inner voice, be a lot of things: the heavy antique furniture calling up troubled fantasies; worry about her grandfather; even disturbance about Anna Beth and the clear tensions in the film crew. But what it was most *likely* to be was that soul-wrenching kiss from Seb Corbel.

How long is it, said the inner voice, since you've been kissed? Have you *ever* been kissed like that?

Jo pushed aside the sheet violently and swung her legs off the bed, as if she could get away from it. She went across to the tall windows and pushed them open almost violently.

As she had discovered earlier, they opened on to a gallery that ran round the courtyard at the height of the first storey. All the grandest rooms opened off the gallery,

the most luxurious being those at the corners. Anna Beth
had the one at the far end of Jo's gallery, a huge 'L'
shape with a view of the formal gardens on one side and
the branches of the courtyard's lemon trees on the other.
A carved wooden staircase ran between the courtyard
and that corner of the gallery.

'Anna Beth's private entrance,' Lisa the wardrobe
mistress had said drily, when she had accompanied Jo
to her room for the measuring session.

The curtains billowed about her as Jo breathed in the
night air. It was scarcely cooler than during the day. She
hesitated for a moment, but everything was silent. She
went restlessly on to the balcony. The air was cooler
outside but there was still no real breeze.

Jo leant both arms on the wooden balustrade that ran
round the first floor. There were a couple of lights still
glowing in the courtyard below. The scent of jasmine
drifted up to her. She felt as if she were the only one
awake. She wondered idly what time it was.

Just like old times, she thought wryly: wakeful and
lonely and still a bit shivery from the dream. Would she
ever get over it? If it didn't leave her in ten years, would
it be with her for the rest of her life?

She shivered again and clasped her arms about herself.
She was reluctant to go back to the magnificent, op-
pressive room. So it was purely by chance that she
glimpsed the movement among the greenery below her.

For a moment Jo froze. Was it a burglar? she wondered, turning over possible courses of action rapidly.
But she dismissed the thought almost immediately as a
soft laugh wafted up to her. No, some member of the
crew who had decided to risk a late night, notwithstanding Seb's punishing schedule, she thought in
amusement. She drew back into the shadows, although

nobody would have been able to see her from the courtyard.

Then she saw that there were people on Anna Beth's staircase. They were talking in whispers, clearly oblivious of the possibility of a watcher.

Chilled, Jo drew back deeper into the shadow of her open windows. But for some reason she could not take her eyes off the shadowy couple on the staircase.

For it was clearly a man and a woman. They were laughing and murmuring. They sounded very happy.

Jo hesitated. As she did so, Anna Beth's unmistakable figure whirled into view. She danced up the stairs in a swirl of bright petticoats, and turned to fling her arms round the man who was behind her. Jo watched, frozen.

She could not really see the man. She could only make out that he was tall and lithe and moved like a dancer. He was wearing a blindingly white shirt which bunched under Anna Beth's fierce fingers as he gathered her to him. Jo heard the girl give a throaty laugh as she pulled his head down towards her. The passion in the embrace was almost tangible.

It was the man who broke it. He flung back his head, laughing. Jo saw the strong throat and hawk-like profile and, for no reason at all, found herself shivering. In the half-light he was demonic. Wild and full of life, he clenched the slim body against the dark strength of his own as if he would absorb the essence of her into himself. Then he bent his head and kissed her, like a snake striking.

It made Jo feel cold. She could feel the challenge coming out of him even across the darkness when he was in another woman's arms, not even aware of her.

How long since you've been kissed? Have you ever been kissed like that?

What's *happening* to me? she thought a little desperately.

Who *was* he? Jo searched her memory and could not recall anyone remotely like him. Surely, this evening, most of the cast and crew had been there?

Suddenly she realised what he reminded her of: a gypsy, down from the high mountain for an hour; free as that high, hot air. And probably, Jo thought while her curtains curled round her in an unexpected breeze, as dangerous as the rocks she had seen on those harsh slopes. She shivered again.

There was another burst of muted laughter. At the end of the balcony the gypsy pounced on the girl, sweeping her off her feet and swinging her round exuberantly so that her toes left the ground. Anna Beth's luxuriant hair fanned out, tangling with his own. Jo had the swift impression that it was of midnight blackness, faintly curling over the deep collar of that white shirt. Then they were gone, Anna Beth pulling him by the hand.

There was not much doubt, thought Jo, where they were going. She felt inexplicably shaken.

She turned and went back into her room. It no longer seemed so stifling. She did not get straight into bed, however. Instead she turned on the dressing-table light and sat in front of the pretty mirror and looked at herself: face too pale and too thin and the dark shadows of overwork all too visible in the shadowed light. That was familiar, but there was something else that wasn't—a tension in the cheekbones, as if she was under strain; and an unmistakable sadness.

Serves you right, Jo told herself wryly, for lurking in shadows watching things that are none of your business.

She leaned forwards, propping her hand on her chin. In less than twelve hours, she thought ruefully, she had bumped her nose on two separate bits of other people's business, what with Simon's crush on Anna Beth, and Anna Beth and her gypsy; to say nothing of Seb Corbel with his unpredictable temper and even more unpredictable amusement.

It's nothing to do with me, she thought, straightening. Nothing at all. I never get involved. And this job isn't going to be any different.

Even to herself, it sounded less than convincing.

The next morning she was up at her usual time, though. In spite of the heat and the strange room, she had slept in the end. The nightmare had not come back but she was aware that her dreams had been disturbed, though she could not now recall the images that had kept her tossing and turning.

She put on shorts and a cotton T-shirt, cotton socks and stout, professional trainers, and let herself quietly out of the great mansion. She had not yet looked at a map but she had a fairly clear idea of where she could run without getting lost.

She set off at a steady jog beside the carriage drive.

The ground was hard as concrete, and uneven. Jo ran lightly, deliberately slowing her pace and minimising the impact of each step as much as she could. She did not want to end up with painful knees or ankles before she even started work.

There was no one about. It was already warm, with just the slight memory of dew to take the edge off it. It would be hazy later, she knew, but now the air was clear as a diamond.

She swung away from the drive, taking a small path in the scrub that soon enough led round an outcrop of rock, hiding the house and drive from view. It curved round the side of the hill, great boulders breaking out of the hillside from time to time. And then she rounded another curve and the hillside fell dramatically away to her left, so that she was on the very edge of the mountain which soared away above her head. It was like running in air.

Jo was exhilarated. For the first time since she had arrived, she felt in harmony with herself. She flung up her arms and her chin and laughed, feeling the high air through her hair like a dangerous caress.

She slowed to a trot, then to a walk; then she perched on one of the boulders and let her eyes scan the valley as it fell away in front of her.

It was beautiful. It was more than beautiful. It had a rugged, challenging magnificence that stirred her blood.

Jo gave a great sigh and relaxed, tipping her head back. The morning sun warmed her face pleasantly, but she could feel its increasing power. After a while, sighing a little, she stood up and began to make her steady way back.

Far below her she could see a thin ribbon of road. There must be some sort of vehicle on it—for she could see a cloud of dust—travelling fast. She grinned, and gave the invisible driver a wave. Then she took the path that led back to the house and left the view and the valley behind her.

When she got back there was still nobody stirring in the main part of the house. Jo showered, and changed into clean shorts and shirt, and went in search of the kitchen.

There were people there, all right. The Spanish girls who had waited at table the other night; a couple of solid matrons pushing purposefully at what looked like

mountains of dough; and a small tough man who seemed
to run the place.

It was he who took one look at Jo, hesitating in the
corner, and came over.

'Good morning, *señorita*. Breakfast? Coffee? Fruit?'

Jo looked at the activity in the kitchen and was
conscience-stricken. 'Could I make some coffee myself?
Instant coffee?'

He looked affronted. People did not drink instant
coffee out of his kitchen, clearly. But he showed her a
saucepan, a range with hotplates and a *cafetière*, and
allowed her to make her own brew once he had ground
the beans for her.

Jo wrinkled her nose in appreciation at the aroma.
'That's wonderful.'

He thawed. He gave her a big cup and asked whether
she had been out.

Jo grinned. 'On a run. My fitness programme. All
part of the job.'

He looked faintly appalled but all he said was, 'Señor
Corbel will be back soon. He went out with the camera
crew of Unit One to look at a site for filming.'

Jo nodded. She was used to the hours that film crews
kept, especially when they were overrunning, and had
been surprised by the lack of movement in the house.

He looked at his watch. 'Señor Corbel wanted
breakfast at six forty-five.'

'I can wait till then,' Jo said, taking the hint.

She poured hot water on to the coffee grounds, picked
up the *cafetière* and cup and took herself out into the
morning light.

The kitchen gave on to what was clearly a working
courtyard. There were buckets and ladders and a small
pile of bricks. There was also a central olive tree with a

stone wall round its base and, in the far corner, what looked like an old well.

She leant her back against the olive tree and sipped at her coffee with a sigh of contentment.

She sat there for thirty minutes or so while the dew slowly evaporated and the mountains ahead became fuzzy with a heat haze. Behind her the kitchen was alive with voices and clattering pans. Nobody emerged from the house, however. The actors and crew were evidently still sleeping.

Jo was enjoying a pleasant feeling of solitude and languorous delight in the day's warmth, when the sound of an engine shattered her daydream.

Her eyes sharpened and she sat up abruptly as a Land Rover bounced through the gates and swept round in a sputter of dust to stop by the well. The driver leaned out of his open window, dust in his hair and on his open-necked shirt, and grinned at her.

'Up early,' Seb Corbel said, amused.

Jo felt herself tense. She did not know why. She met his eyes levelly. 'Likewise.'

He got out and strolled across to her. As before, his every move was lithe and precise. It was oddly at variance with his lazy manner. For a moment she was reminded of last night's gypsy. Except that Seb Corbel would not lose cool for anything, Jo thought; though maybe Anna Beth could bring him closer to it than others.

His shadow engulfed her. Jo had to curb an instinct to stand up and defy that towering presence. Seb's eyes narrowed. But all he said was, 'All part of the job. I've been looking at locations for the duel. The place Nick had found was too dangerous. And anyway, we couldn't get a decent perspective of the mountains.'

It was Jo's turn to grin. She had met directors before who said they were worried about their actors' safety but really meant they were dissatisfied with the picture they got.

'So you've found the mountains and maybe it won't be any more dangerous?' she asked drily.

Seb dropped down beside her. 'Do you worry?' he asked, looking at her curiously.

'About the danger?' Jo shook her head, using the movement to disguise the fact that she moved slightly away from him on the bench, so that the unexpectedly muscular thigh was no longer just touching her own. 'No. It's my job to minimise it of course. And live with what I can't avoid.'

His eyes, for all the lazy manner, were unexpectedly sharp. Jo suddenly found herself blushing. There was a speculative light in the brown eyes that said he knew she had moved away and was wondering what might lie behind her action.

She tensed. But he did not challenge her; instead, he stretched, putting his hands behind his head and arching his long spine.

'How did you get into it?' he asked idly of the sky, flexing his shoulders.

Jo let out a relieved breath that she hoped he did not notice. 'Stunting? Accident, really. I was on holiday in Ireland when a crew on location wanted somebody to ride a horse for them, and I could. I enjoyed it. I didn't know what I was going to do with my life. So...' She shrugged.

He stopped stretching and turned to her. 'So it was pure chance? Going where the wind blew you?' He was thoughtful. 'That's impressive.'

Jo looked away. It had not quite been like that. She had been sixteen and close to desperate.

'What would you have done if the wind hadn't blown you in that direction?' Seb asked casually.

That, thought Jo, was a very nasty thought indeed. She had been out of her wits trying to work something out.

'I honestly don't know. My—my mother was talking about finishing-school. I'd have hated that.'

He looked momentarily surprised. 'I thought finishing-school was a thing of the past.'

'Not at all. They're very useful places for people who don't mind how much they pay to get rid of their children,' Jo said, unwisely.

There was a small pause. Then Seb said, 'Ah.'

She stood up, half turning away from him. She was angry with herself for having revealed so much. She didn't usually. She must, she realised, be very careful with Seb Corbel. He had a knack, with his lazy silence, of making you say more than you meant.

Jo set out to retrieve the position, her voice careful. 'I was a displaced child, you see. After the divorce my parents both had real families with their new partners.' It was the truth, but not the whole truth. She did not think about the whole truth now, ever.

'It happens,' Seb said neutrally.

'Yes. And both sets are stinking rich,' Jo said dispassionately. 'I never wanted for anything.'

Except a home; and encouragement; and security. Grandpa had provided what he could, of course, but he had quarrelled with them and money had always gone through his hands like water. Jo had never known when the bailiffs would arrive. Still, it was better than the Mayfair flat, or the sprawling villa in St Tropez.

'Then you're luckier than most,' Seb said briskly. He too stood up. 'Do you want coffee?'

He brought a fresh pot out and set it down on the ground while he unlaced two mugs from his fingers. He looked up at her.

'Sit down, for heaven's sake. I've never known such an unrestful woman.'

To her own slight surprise, Jo was amused. She laughed and did as he ordered, shrugging.

'That's better.' He looked her over assessingly. 'Was that you on the high path this morning?'

She was startled by the abrupt question. 'Yes, I expect so.' She remembered the dust cloud in the valley road. 'You must have very good eyesight.'

Seb shook his head. 'I had binoculars. I was looking for shots.' He dealt with the coffee swiftly and gave her a mug of it. 'Do you run every morning?'

'When I can.'

'To stay in condition?'

'Partly. But I enjoy it, too.'

He sat on the earth, crossing his legs. It meant he was at her feet, looking almost directly into her face.

'So you really enjoy your work?' he mused.

Jo laughed again. 'Sometimes. Sometimes not. Who doesn't? I didn't enjoy being dragged along a beach in a sodden wetsuit.'

Seb looked amused. He knew the film she was referring to. 'But the other stuff? You enjoy that? You do the lot, don't you?'

Jo thought irritably that he must know exactly what was in her repertoire since that was ostensibly why he had asked for her.

'I swim,' she said evenly. 'I ride. I ski. I climb. And I bounce off things.'

'Quite a list. How did you put it together?' He was gravity itself.

Jo looked away from those too-intent eyes. It was horridly as if he were looking into her soul and seeing the reflected memories she wanted so hard to forget.

It had been the same every holiday. When a boarding-school term had ended she was collected by one or other impatient parent, and on the ride home the conversation would follow a pattern.

'Have you thought what you'd like to do, darling? What about riding with Veronica? There's a good residential place in Wexford...'

Tennis in Portugal. Skiing in Verbier. Scuba-diving in the West Indies. Her holidays had been a schoolgirl's dream. When she'd gone back at the start of term her friends had been frankly envious. It was so sophisticated, going off on your own to learn how to do all those dashing, daring things. Their parents had insisted that they still went on the boring family holidays to the beach, in by ten and no unaccompanied overnight trips with friends. How they had envied Jo her freedom. How terrific her glamorous parents must be.

How long did it take to realise you were not wanted? How long did it take to make sure that you didn't care any more? And took care that you wouldn't care ever again?

Jo said with an effort, 'I devoted my adolescence to it.'

Seb was relaxed. He looked almost as if he was half asleep. Jo did not trust him an inch.

'But you weren't preparing to be a stunt woman. So why? Did you want to be an Olympic medallist?'

Jo looked at him steadily. 'Since you must know, I've never been in the Olympic team. That wouldn't have been a very kind question if I did want to be a medallist.'

He laughed. 'I'm not very kind. Did you?'

'No.'

He was not at all put out by her short tone. 'So why?'

Jo shrugged. 'I enjoyed it. I may not be a natural athlete, but I like the open air.'

That was true, as far as it went. But he still sat there, still lazy, but still definitely demanding an answer. She searched for something.

'And I like doing things well,' Jo said at last.

'Ah,' he said again in a satisfied tone. Then, with a complete change of manner that would have left her gasping if she had not already been suspicious of him, he sat up and said crisply, 'Do you think you're going to be able to do this part well?'

Jo took a minute to think about it. She had read the script, of course. Last night she had gone through it again, looking at her own part with particular attention. But, until they actually went into rehearsal and she knew what the director wanted precisely in each scene, she had only the haziest idea of what it might entail.

'It depends what you're looking for,' she said at last. 'Technically, I can do it. At least, as it's written.' There was a faint question in her voice. Seb ignored it.

'What about the duel?'

One of the big set-pieces was a duel between the disguised heroine and the villain. Jo shrugged.

'I can fence.'

He looked at her over the rim of the cup again. 'We've got Carlos Andrade for Henry.'

Jo gave a soundless whistle. Andrade was a world medallist. 'As we've just established, I'm not Olympic class.'

Seb shrugged. 'That doesn't matter. Nobody would expect the girl to hold her own for long.' He grinned suddenly. 'And you're supposed to lose.'

'The story of my life,' Jo said lightly.

He gave her a quick look under those devilish eye-brows. It was only then that she thought how prophetic it sounded.

CHAPTER THREE

THE others emerged during the next hour. Jo noticed that Seb resumed his abstracted air as soon as any of them approached him. In particular, Anna Beth. When she appeared, looking stunning in tight jewel-coloured trousers and shirt, he became so vague as to be bordering on, in Jo's view, a ham actor's version of the absent-minded professor. It intrigued her.

But she did not have much time to think about Seb Corbel and his eccentricities. She had to be fitted into the costumes of her injured predecessor. And after that she had to go and rehearse.

Jo worked hard all morning, and went to snatch a quick lunch with the others, taking the script with her. That afternoon she had to rehearse a headlong dash to stop the coach, ending with her falling off the horse.

Miguel Ramirez dropped into the chair beside her as she read her way through the scene again over lunch. His own plate was piled high with cold meats and fish in exotic sauces. He peered over her shoulder.

'Oh, the highway raid,' he said, his mouth full. 'That's going to be hell. You know they've had a fight about it already?'

'Fight?' Jo was bewildered. 'Who?'

'Seb and the Queen of Sheba,' Miguel said drily. 'She wants to do it herself. She says her contract allows her to do her own riding.'

Jo tensed. But she said, casually enough, 'Surely Anna Beth is much too valuable a property to be allowed to fall off a horse?'

47

'At least until filming is over,' Miguel agreed. He gave her an odd look as he forked up another substantial mouthful. 'Do you ever mind?'

Jo stared. 'Mind what?'

He shrugged. 'Oh, being an expendable bag of bones so the leading lady can stay immaculate?'

She laughed. 'That's my job.'

He was dissatisfied. 'But don't you ever get frustrated? Don't you want to get out there and act your own part? See your own name in lights?'

Before she could answer she felt an odd sensation, as if someone had a training rein on her and was forcing her to bring her head round. It was unnerving. She tensed her shoulders and refused to turn, looking steadily ahead of her. She was very nearly certain she knew who it was.

'Oh, Seb, there you are,' she heard Miguel say. 'I was looking for you.'

How could he do it to her? Did he do it deliberately? Did he know he did it at all?

What is happening to me? she thought again, scared.

'Have you thought about the thunderstorm?' Miguel went on. Then, 'Seb?'

Jo did look up then. She could not help herself.

'Yes,' he said to Miguel absently.

He was looking down at her. The brown eyes were full of undisguised speculation. How much had he overheard? she thought in sudden alarm. Hastily she looked away.

Although he was answering Miguel, she could feel his eyes, almost like a caress, on her averted cheek. And Miguel was watching them both. She pushed her plate away.

'Time I was back at work,' she said, nodding impartially at both of them.

She walked away slowly, though her every instinct was to run. She knew he was watching her, too. She had never felt so conscious of her body—of the length of her legs, the proud carriage of her head. She knew he was watching, and it was only by a supreme effort of will that she managed neither to run nor to turn and look back at him.

Once out of sight, it was a different matter. Jo flung back her head and took to her heels as if the devil were after her.

This, she told herself, has got to stop. I am working for the man, for heaven's sake. I can't go into an adolescent fit every time I clap eyes on him. But she did not go back.

When she stopped running, her lungs heaved. She felt ashamed. After all, he was only a man. And so far, for all his fearsome reputation, he had been nothing but pleasant to her. If she felt as if his eyes were lasers, cutting deep into her flesh and uncovering secrets she had been carefully burying for years, that was pure neurosis on her part.

'You're going barmy, my girl,' she told herself grimly. 'Just like Uncle Jerry said. Getting into a flap about a director who doesn't know you exist. And,' thinking of last night, 'picking a fight with an actress you *know* is bad news. What you need is a good dose of perspective.'

She looked down at the shooting-script scenes, still clenched in her hand. She began to laugh a little. The answer was there, after all. As she had told them she was here to work; and her work had to be prepared, even if she did not have lines to learn.

She squared her shoulders and went to look at the horse she would be riding.

Simon caught her up on her way out of the house, and went with her. 'How are things going?' he asked brightly.

Jo looked at him. He had probably heard about the little scene with Anna Beth at the dinner table last night, though he had said nothing to her about it.

He looked away. 'Anna Beth's on tenterhooks at the moment,' he said.

Jo shrugged.

'Don't get the wrong idea about her,' Simon said earnestly. 'She's a very caring person.'

Jo said nothing. She had a fair idea of what sort of person Anna Beth Arden was, and she did not think she was likely to agree with Simon on the subject. He was clearly besotted.

'Seb's being an absolute *pig*,' he burst out, 'picking on her all the time. Criticising.'

'You surprise me,' Jo said with truth.

'Oh, I know he looks as if he's too lazy to pick up a shooting script for himself. But he's an absolute fiend when he gets going,' Simon assured her.

'Oh? Eats actors for breakfast, does he?' Jo asked, amused.

'You wait,' Simon told her. 'You won't laugh when he tears into *you*. And he will. I had poor Anna Beth in tears last night...' He stopped in sudden confusion.

Tactfully Jo looked the other way. But she was intrigued. So Simon had been comforting Anna Beth, had he? Could he possibly be the gypsy figure she had glimpsed down the gallery last night? It seemed unlikely. He did not have the presence; the vitality that had hit her like a forcefield even at thirty paces. Yet—who else could it be?

Remembering the scene she had witnessed, she shivered. She looked away from him. If it was Simon, she found she did not want to know.

They reached the stables. Jo found a lad who understood more English than she did Spanish. He took them to a loose box where a glossy bay was gazing placidly across the yard.

Jo gave the beast an apple which was well received by horse and lad alike. Then she began to talk to the creature, patting its nose with dawning affection. The horse snorted in a friendly way and nuzzled after more apples.

'*That's* OK,' she said in relief after a few more minutes. She scratched behind his ear, saying goodbye, and saw Simon watching her. 'Sometimes people think that because you do stunts you're a rodeo rider,' she explained ruefully. 'You wouldn't believe some of the savages I've been offered in the past.'

The lad grinned. 'Salome,' he said.

'What?' Simon was as startled as Jo.

'Salome.' And he gestured to them to follow.

Salome was beautiful. She clearly had palomino blood, with a golden sheen to her coat and an aristocratic nose. She was also tossing her head and snorting in a way that was anything but friendly. Her eyes were dark and liquid and, at the moment, bright with temper.

The lad scratched her nose and she tossed her head up as if throwing him away. Not a bit annoyed, he grinned even more.

'Salome,' he said proudly.

'So I see.' Jo walked up to the loose box and looked the horse in the eye. 'You're in a mean mood, aren't you, beautiful?' she said softly.

The horse watched her.

'I say, you're not going to try riding that one, are you?' Simon said, suddenly nervous.

Jo shook her head. 'She's a killer. I don't expect I'm strong enough. Anyway, you'd need to get to know this one and I don't have the time.'

They thanked the lad and left the stables.

Simon said curiously, 'What do you mean, you don't have the time? We're into overrun already. There's no end date for filming.'

'Not for you maybe.' Jo pushed a hand through her short hair, suddenly aware of how tired she was of dashing from job to job. 'But I've got a full schedule.'

Simon said simply, 'Why? I mean it's bloody well paid. Surely you can afford a break? I'd have thought you'd need one: all that flinging yourself around,' he added with feeling.

'Oh, I need one,' Jo said grimly.

There were footsteps behind them. Once again she felt that magnetic awareness flow over her, as if some planet had suddenly fixed itself in her horizon and was pulling her. She stiffened, fighting it.

'Need what?' drawled Seb Corbel, coming out of a walled gateway.

Simon, thought Jo furiously, was obviously used to his master's habit of creeping up on people.

'Hi, Seb,' he said without visible surprise. 'A holiday, by the sound of it.'

Seb gave her a complicated look and his mouth quirked. 'Not on my time,' he said. 'Nor until this one's in the can.'

Jo glared. 'I never suggested it.'

He gave her a lazy grin. 'Well, don't. Time is money in this business, and I've dangerously overspent on both.'

Simon said, 'This afternoon...'

'No point,' Seb returned. He was quite pleasant, but there was a slight weariness in his tone which suggested to Jo that he had said this a number of times before to Simon.

'The light won't be with us for long enough. I want them out on the hill at six tomorrow.' He paused and then said with great deliberation, '*All* of them.'

Simon's fair skin flushed easily. He was slightly pink now. 'Seb, if people are ill...'

'If people are ill, they go to hospital,' Seb said gently. 'Otherwise they work like everyone else.'

'But——'

'Stop worrying.' The drawl was more exaggerated. 'I don't think you'll have any problem.'

For no reason that Jo could see, Simon flushed even darker. The look he sent Seb smouldered with resentment. He said stiffly, 'Then I'd better go and get the running order distributed.'

'Do that,' Seb said amiably.

And Simon turned a shoulder and stalked away as if he had just issued a dueller's challenge. Or received one.

For a moment Seb looked after him, his mouth unexpectedly grim. Then he shrugged, and turned back to Jo. 'Any problems?'

Looking after Simon in her turn, Jo said drily, 'With the stunts?'

'Been weeping on your shoulder, has he?' Seb drawled. 'Ignore him.'

As that was exactly what Jo had resolved to do, it was quite unreasonable that she should be annoyed by Seb's telling her to do exactly that. But she was. He saw her frown and seemed amused.

Jo said stiffly, 'I'm not sure when you want me.'

Seb sighed. 'No. You wouldn't be. That's all part of what Simon is losing hold of. You should have been there before lunch.'

'Oh,' said Jo, her sympathy for Simon dwindling sharply. She hated to look unprofessional.

Seb sighed and pushed a hand through his dark hair. 'Don't worry. As it was we had so many retakes, we wouldn't have got to you anyway. But we will this afternoon.'

It sounded like a vow.

Jo said, startled. 'But I haven't rehearsed.'

Seb looked impatient. 'We'll go over it on the ground. It's not *Hamlet, Prince of Denmark*, for heaven's sake. All you've got to is fall over and keep your face out of sight.'

Jo drew a long breath. She had met similar attitudes from other directors, but she could not remember one who had come out and said it so blatantly.

She gave Seb a glacial smile and said sweetly, 'As you pointed out, it's your time and your money. If you want to waste both, it's up to you.' And she turned her back on him and walked—no, marched—away. Behind her, she was almost certain that she heard a soft laugh.

In fact, contrary to her expectations and experience, the afternoon's filming went like clockwork. As a director, Seb was relaxed but clear and decisive in his instructions. And he obviously had a very clear idea of how he wanted the scene to go. In her Elizabethan breeches, ruffled shirt and padded jacket, Jo concentrated on staying as cool as possible, which was not very. They had the little sequence finished in three takes. After the last one, as she rose from the dusty ground, brushing down her breeches, there was a spontaneous round of applause from the crew.

Jo looked up, hesitating.

Bill Hamilton, the actor who had joined her in the sequence, grinned at her and gave her a quick hug. 'Take a medal,' he said.

Jo looked back at the cameras and the lighting gear, with their operators still clapping, and said blankly, *'Me?'*

'You, indeed. Do you know the average number of takes per scene so far?' But he said it under his breath.

Seb came over to them. His face was impassive. Unlike his crew, he was certainly not about to fall on her neck, Jo thought. Not that she wanted him to, of course. Nevertheless it was galling not to have him admit, as the others were openly doing, that she had done a good job.

The auburn wig that turned her into a substitute for Anna Beth was tight across her temples. She put up fingers to ease it. She saw him watch the movement.

She was suddenly conscious of how she must look, dishevelled and hot from her exertions. There was something in his expression that unsettled her. Her eyes slid away from his.

Seb said quietly, 'We'll look at it this evening. Now, Bill, back to the apricot tree and we'll see if we can catch up with scene fifty-one. Don't need you any more, Jo.'

Dismissed, she went back to the mobile dressing-room. She was too experienced to pull the wig off, though it was suffocatingly tight, and the girls in the caravan flew to help her take it off as soon as she got inside the door.

They, too, she found, were impressed. They helped her out of the heavy costume, hanging it carefully. Jo got back into her own shorts and shirt.

'Of course, *she's* off for the day,' one of them said. She was a pretty American girl, filling in the vacation doing a job that had, apparently, turned out to be less glamorous than she expected.

Jo was leaning forwards, brushing her own soft dark hair. 'She?'

'Anna Beth. Normally she goes and watches the shooting, even when she's not involved.'

Jo sat up. 'Oh?'

'That's why it's all taking so long, I guess,' Sue said with the forthrightness of one who was going to be off in a few weeks. 'She goes and hangs round Seb like a groupie, and she's always getting in the way.'

Jo sat back and looked at her face in the mirror above the compact dressing-table. 'Interesting,' she said thoughtfully.

'He can't pack her off, because she's the star. And she has money in it,' said the cynical Sue.

Her companion, older and more professional, gave a snort. 'Her husband's got money in it. And Seb Corbel had better be careful if he wants to keep it.'

Jo's eyebrows rose. But the two needed no encouragement, this was clearly a long-standing contention.

'There's nothing in it. He's just nice to her. He has to be. You know what she's like, Lisa.'

'I know what Seb's like too,' Lisa said.

'Now that's not fair——'

'They're two of a kind.' Lisa was ruthless. 'He's been loving them and leaving them for as long as I can remember. And that makes him even more of a challenge for Anna Beth. They both want to get the upper hand, and they don't care what they do to get it: overspend, mess up the movie, mess up some poor kid's life...' She stopped abruptly. 'I've seen it all before,' she finished.

Jo said, 'If it's his own fault that the thing's so over schedule, why is Corbel complaining?'

Sue looked almost as if she would cry. Lisa gave her an impatient look. A bad case of hero-worship, Jo deduced.

'It's not that simple. You know what it's like.'

Jo rather thought she did. 'Has Anna Beth been watching the filming when these accidents have occurred? The stunts, I mean.'

Lisa gave her a swift, comprehending look.

Sue said, 'And the others.'

Jo stared.

'It isn't just the stunt people who have had accidents,' Sue reported. 'There was a sound man. And I don't know how many of the continuity people. And Linda Lavell, who played the mother.'

Jo straightened.

'We seem to be accident prone,' Lisa said carefully. 'You'd better watch your step.'

It was Sue's turn to snort. 'We're only accident prone when Anna Beth's about.'

Jo walked back to the main house very thoughtfully.

The next day went well, in spite of Jo's uneasiness. Anna Beth returned from her day away, glowing. Jo avoided her. But it hardly seemed necessary. Anna Beth was in a golden mood.

Remembering the dark figure in the night, Jo had an uncomfortable feeling that she knew who Anna Beth had been with and what had given her that look of shining exuberance. She hoped that it did not mean trouble for the film. Try as she would, Jo could not put out of her mind that image. Even in the shadows, across the gallery, he had seemed to her equally dominating and dangerous. And she could understand, too, how Anna Beth was drawn to that dangerous presence. Even Jo had felt the pull of that magnetism, so that it stayed with her, at the edge of her imagination, keeping her on edge and defensive.

Seb noticed it.

'Can't wait to get away, can you, Jo?' he mocked.

It was the evening of her first full day, and she was dust-stained and weary. He caught her up as she walked to the Land Rover in which she had travelled.

Jo said edgily, 'Are you complaining?'

He gave her a sideways glance. His drawl became more pronounced. 'Why should I? If it gets it in the can fast, it has to be a good thing. I'm just curious.'

'Curious?'

He stopped her with a hand on her arm, and turned her round to face him. 'Why?' he asked softly.

Jo bit her lip. She said carefully, 'I think maybe Anna Beth makes me nervous.'

The sleepy gaze did not change. 'A professional like you?' Seb teased softly.

Jo shrugged. 'Everyone has an Achilles heel.'

'Now there I believe you,' Seb said unexpectedly. He gave an odd laugh. 'But I don't believe you're worried about your work. You're much too cool a lady. No, there has to be something else.'

'Does there?' Jo's voice was not encouraging.

Seb's hand tightened on her upper arm. 'Oh, yes. You've been like a cat on hot bricks ever since you got here.' He looked at her searchingly. 'Was your agent right? Is it because of some damned prejudice against me?'

Jo released her arm and took a step backwards. She felt oddly breathless. Beneath the soft voice there was a lick of anger. She said, 'I don't know what you're talking about.'

Seb's look was enigmatic. 'Don't you?'

He reached out very slowly and ran a finger down the side of her face to her jaw, stopping where the pulse was racing at the base of her throat. Jo froze.

She was not prepared and she did not have time to control her instincts. She knew that she would have gone perfectly white. It was an old fear. She could feel the clamminess of her skin. He would see that.

The brown eyes were keen but he let his hand fall slowly. 'Don't you?' he said again.

Jo felt all her muscles lock.

'Whatever you're afraid of,' Seb Corbel said softly, 'it's not filming.'

Jo gave a little laugh that broke in the middle. In one way, of course, he was right. The nightmare had nothing to do with anyone here. It was ingrained. She would carry it around with her for the rest of her life. But she was used to it. And she was not used to the tensions that assaulted her from every side on this film.

With a great effort she shrugged. 'If that's what you want to believe...'

Seb forced her eyes to meet his. 'One day,' he said, not much above a whisper. 'One day, you're going to tell me.' For once he did not sound lazy.

But Jo did not have the time to worry about it. Because the next day everything began to go wrong.

The first thing that happened was a change in the running order, which meant that she was not on the set when she should have been. Seb was drawlingly insulting. Simon said, swiftly and not very convincingly, that it was his fault, and Seb waved the subject away.

Then they had five takes before Jo realised that what she had been told to do was not what Seb wanted. Anna Beth, watching from her canvas chair beside him, smiled kindly. But Seb said nothing.

He gave Jo a crooked smile after the last take, as she eyed him with trepidation. He would have been justified in a mild fit of temper, she acknowledged.

'I'm a philosopher,' he drawled, reading her mind.

Later, Jo was to make a dive off a rock into the lake. It was a spectacular dive, though in fact the rock was not as high as the camera angles were designed to make it appear.

Simon came over after a conference at the canvas chairs and said to her, 'Seb wants it to look as if she's afraid. As if she's not going to be able to do it. Can you...?'

Jo nodded. She had sized up the terrain and the lake earlier. It would not be too difficult, she thought, to run along the top of the cliff, appear to lose her footing and then uncurl into a proper dive as she fell.

She was the only person involved in the scene. Simon had alotted a full three hours to the take, so the others were shopping, or snoozing by the swimming-pool. Anna Beth Arden was at the lake, of course, sitting cross-legged with her cheek resting against the leg of Seb's empty canvas chair.

Seb himself did not sit down at all during takes or after them. But from time to time he passed the chair and touched her hair; Anna Beth would look up with a radiant smile when he did, Jo saw.

Jo was wearing the heavy velvet breeches again, but she had been allowed to discard the jacket. The shirt was full and frilled and would be a nuisance in the water, but at least it was relatively cool.

Seb briefed her in the economical phrases she had come to expect.

'The top of the cliff. Along to where the chalk cross is,' he said, indicating a mark on the ground that, as he and the camera crew had worked out, gave the most striking contrast of perspectives. 'Then over. Start your run when I signal.'

Jo nodded. For some reason she could not quite understand, she was nervous, although it was well within her capabilities.

Seb walked away. He was sitting with the nearest camera, but it was still several hundred yards away. Jo shivered.

He turned; raised his arm; and as it dropped she began to run.

As she had already agreed with Seb, she ran fast, head down, looking over her shoulder twice, in two rapid movements that would blur her features on the screen.

As the cliff edge got nearer she managed to stagger a little as Simon had told her. She thought she heard someone call out but she knew that Seb would be furious if she allowed herself to be distracted. She gave one last, frantic look behind her, did a quarter turn on the chalk mark and went lurching over the cliff in a bundle of flying arms and hair.

She uncurled in the air quickly, tucking her head in and drawing a deep breath just in time. Then she was cutting cleanly through the still water, her body one arrow-slim line.

Good, thought Jo, surfacing in a more leisurely fashion. She struck out for the rocks with easy strokes, as the muslin shirt and trailing wig clung to her back and arms. Very good indeed. Even Seb Corbel would be pleased with that.

She climbed out and splashed round the rocks to where she had left a towel and robe. She stripped and dried her limbs, bundling up the clothes before going back to the others.

She was climbing the path up from the lake when she heard feet. Someone was pelting down the stony track at an irresponsible pace. Rounding a knoll, she stopped dead.

'What the *hell*,' demanded Seb Corbel, no longer philosophical, 'do you think you're doing?'

His face was grey under the sweat and dust, and his eyes were narrowed to slits of fury.

Jo's mouth fell open.

Seb reached her. She could see now that the brown eyes were dark and cold as graphite. The laid-back director might never have existed.

He grabbed her by the shoulders with hands that hurt. Her bundle of clothing fell with a plop on to the spiny plants beside the track. Jo made a distracted move towards them and found herself pulled up hard against Seb.

'I didn't *believe* it . . .' he ground out.

He was too close. Her pulses began to shriek that he was too close. The nightmare hovered. Jo stared desperately up into the cold and blazing eyes only inches away, and found her head beginning to swim.

'What did I say to you?' He shook her a little. 'No heroics. No showing-off. Only you can't resist it, can you? Have you ever heard of a stunt that isn't a world record breaker?'

Jo said, 'I don't understand.'

'Don't you? When I went over with you, this morning, exactly what I wanted, you said you understood. Then you just had to go and pull that damned stupid stunt . . .'

And he shook her again as if he could not find words to express himself.

Jo collected herself. 'Now look here——' she began.

'No, *you* look. Do you know what I thought—back there, when you decided to go for stardom?' Seb said between his teeth.

'What the devil are you talking about?' Jo strove without success to free herself.

'I thought you'd fallen. I thought you'd really fallen. I thought you'd—hurt yourself.'

Light dawned. Jo stopped struggling. If he'd been watching and hadn't realised her trip was deliberate, he must have thought she'd gone over the side unprepared. In which case he must have thought she'd be killed. There were rocks in the lake, and the point at which she went off the cliff had been very carefully chosen.

She said, 'Didn't you see I'd gone over where the chalk mark was?'

'I wasn't looking through a camera lens, was I?' Seb said furiously. 'I saw you weren't running straight—and that wasn't in the screenplay either. I—thought you'd had a brainstorm.'

Jo said slowly, 'I thought that was what you wanted.'

Seb howled with rage. 'How many times do I have to tell you? This isn't an adventure movie. I don't want a legend. Anyway, I wouldn't have thought the best in the world needed that kind of publicity.'

'I don't,' said Jo shortly.

'Then will you please remember it?' he said equally shortly.

Jo set her teeth. She didn't understand. But something was dubious about Simon's last-minute instructions. Looking at the furious man in front of her, however, Jo realised that this was not the time to accuse Simon. He was in enough trouble with Seb as it was. And she could not be certain that he had not genuinely misunderstood Seb's intentions.

She said soothingly, 'I didn't mean to upset you——'

'Upset?'

Jo began to get angry. 'I was trying to do my best for your damned film,' she flashed at him. 'I thought——'

'Well, don't!' Seb shouted at her. 'We'll all be a lot healthier if you just do as you're told. As you're paid to.'

'With pleasure,' hissed Jo, as angry as he was. 'Now let me go.'

Seb seemed to have forgotten that he was still holding her. He looked down at her for a moment as if he had suddenly woken up to the fact. Then he gave an odd sound between a laugh and a groan, and tightened his arms around her as his head came down.

From nowhere the nightmare whirled up and engulfed Jo.

She heard herself say, 'No,' in an anguished whimper. Or she thought she said it. In this nightmare, as so often before, she felt helpless and voiceless. She heard the man's thunderous breathing; shrank from the hard hands as if they would grind her bones to dust. Jo could feel his anger beating at her like a flame. Behind her, and to her left, the perilous path tilted and swayed.

She gave an ugly sound that was pure animal terror and fell into the swirling landscape.

CHAPTER FOUR

THERE was noise all around her. Jo fought her way up to consciousness muzzily, aware of something wrong. The nightmare always came in sinister silence. Why all these voices? And running feet, as if she were in an adventure movie. She turned her head, and found that one part of the nightmare at least had not changed: the unknown man's laboured breathing.

Panic filled her throat. She gave a whimper. It was a dream, she told herself as she had done before. Only a dream. She would be all right if only she could wake up.

She pushed her hands against an oddly warm pillow.

'Careful,' said someone.

The voices changed—came closer. Bewildered, Jo opened her eyes.

She was not in bed. Held precariously against a muscular chest, she was being carried up a steep slope. Spiny trees and bushes plucked at her. Ahead and up the slope people were coming towards them in a rush, calling out. Jo's heart lurched and she grasped convulsively at the man who was carrying her.

'Careful,' Seb said again. His voice sounded odd.

Jo turned her head. He was breathing hard. But he was climbing the rock-strewn path with long steady strides. Close to, she could see the laughter lines on his face. Which was odd, too, she thought in the detachment of her dream state, since he was not remotely smiling. In fact he looked almost fierce.

Above them someone was calling, 'Seb, is she all right?'

Then she heard Simon's voice. 'Jo. Jo.'

She must have shifted her weight, because Seb's hands tightened round her. He said, 'If you value your life, don't squirm.'

Jo could feel the hurried rise and fall of his chest where he held her against him. It was an intimate, uncomfortable sensation. The last wisps of the dream disappeared, and with them her composure.

'I can walk,' she said sharply.

He gave her a look of contempt. 'I doubt it.'

Jo began to struggle in his arms. Then she caught sight of the drop to the beach below and went unnaturally still. 'You'll kill us both,' she said, holding herself rigid. Even her lips barely moved.

The cold eyes glinted down at her. 'Think of the headlines,' he said affably, not checking his stride. '"World-Famous Stunt Girl and Director in Death Dive."' His eyes were not affable.

Jo glared at him. 'Headlines I can do without.'

'Really?' His drawl was a careful insult.

'Yes, really.' She was almost shouting. 'What do I need publicity for? Stunts are supposed to be done anonymously. What good will it do my career if I lose my anonymity?'

His eyes narrowed. 'You could be contemplating a change in career.'

Jo looked over his arm at the expanse of gorse and rock that fell away to the water's edge. She did not give much for their chances if Seb missed his footing. And he did not seem to be concentrating too hard on the difficulties of the path. She repressed a shudder.

'I'm thinking of it right now.'

He did not answer. The path, in one of its sudden swoops, had turned sharply back on itself and they were facing a bare slope that to Jo's jaundiced eye looked set at a sixty-degree angle at least. Seb shifted her so that he held her more securely, bent forwards slightly, and took the slope at a scrambling run. Jo clutched at him, her face pressed against his neck.

At the top he stopped, his chest rising and falling hard. He looked down at her. Jo released her grip and stared up at him, disconcerted. He showed no sign of letting her go.

Then the others came round the corner.

Very slowly, it seemed, Seb lowered her to her feet.

'Are you OK?' That was Simon. He looked anxious, Jo saw, as she tore her eyes away from Seb's.

Before she had time to answer, Seb said cuttingly, 'So OK that she passed out down there.' And he jerked his head in the direction of the beach.

Although he had allowed her to stand, he still had an arm round her. It felt like an iron bar.

Simon's eyes flickered. 'Jo?'

'Just a bit winded,' she said carefully. She did not look at Seb, but she felt the iron bar tighten.

Miguel said enthusiastically, 'That was a hell of a dive.'

Seb reverted to laziness. 'Yes, we should have made up some time, there,' he drawled. He looked down at Jo, the brown eyes glinting. 'Are you always a one-take wonder?'

Jo shook her head. She was shaken. The difference between the furious man on the path and this one was too great. 'Luck,' she murmured.

Seb said, 'Then while the luck and the light are with us, let's use them. Move, my children.'

Jo went slowly back to the caravan where the costumes were kept during the day. She was going to have to talk to Simon. He had just made her look seriously unprofessional. No matter how much she sympathised with him, she could not let him get away with that.

The girls who helped her out of the sopping wig confirmed her feeling that Simon was infatuated with Anna Beth.

'And maybe he's not the only one,' said Sue, the younger of them. She did not seem happy about it.

Lisa, her senior, shrugged. 'Seb always has someone around. It's not serious. Not like the Curtis boy. No one's going to break Seb Corbel's heart for him.'

Sue sighed. 'He's out of his depth,' she said. 'He thinks he's St George and it's up to him to look out for Anna Beth. He's sweet.'

'He's an idiot,' said practical Lisa, with a snort.

Looking in the mirror, Jo fluffed up her dark hair, released from the wig, and thought about the stories she had heard about the director. Between them, he and Anna Beth Arden could hurt Simon Curtis pretty badly. She became all the more determined to shield Simon from Corbel's wrath if she could.

There was a knock on the caravan door.

'Revised schedule for Miss Page,' said someone, unseen.

Sue went to the door and came back with a typed running sheet. She handed it to Lisa who cast her eye down it and whistled.

'Seb's on a roll,' she said lightly. 'Keep the animals working while the performance is going well, I suppose. Going to be a tough day.'

And she handed it over to Jo.

Sue said nervously, 'Lisa—the rags. I forgot them. That is, I thought Simon said . . . What on earth are we going to do?'

Jo glanced down at the paper. They must, she realised, be talking about the last scene. She was supposed to jump out of a tree in front of the hero. It was quite a late scene, and the heroine had been on the run for some time in the plot.

Jo chuckled. 'I'm surprised she's wearing anything at all by that time,' she said drily. 'After climbing mountains and diving into lakes for a week.'

Lisa snorted with amusement. 'Perhaps you could suggest that to Seb. It might solve the problem,' she suggested.

But between them the girls contrived something. It got an indifferent glance from Seb, and a wolf-whistle from Bill Hamilton that had the sound man jumping up and clapping his hands over ears that had received it at full volume.

'Oh, *boy*,' said Bill with feeling. 'Just as well our little Southern belle isn't here to see *that*.'

Jo opened her eyes wide at him. 'Is that a compliment?' she asked gently.

'Believe it,' Bill said enthusiastically. 'Where have you been all my life?'

She grinned. 'Dressed,' she said with composure.

He shook his head. 'Pity.' He sent Seb a quick look and then lowered his voice. 'Still, it'll be no bad thing if Anna Beth doesn't find out. Stunt girls aren't supposed to be gorgeous. And she's already miffed because Simon told her Seb said you were a wonder. Prat that he is. She can get—er—difficult when someone else is centre stage. Or so she thinks.'

Jo, too, looked at Seb. He was talking to Miguel. 'I've stunted for her before,' she said casually.

Bill sent her a quick look. 'Before or after she was *Newsworld*'s cover story?'

Jo said, 'Was that her great breakthrough? I didn't realise.'

'About three months after she married the owner,' Bill informed her neutrally.

Jo pulled a face. 'Ah. I didn't know that either. This would have been about—oh, eighteen months ago.'

'Before, then. But only just before. She was well and truly on the way up then.'

'Yes. I could see that,' Jo agreed.

Bill hesitated and then said, 'You know that her husband has a lot of money invested in this film?'

'I—had gathered. Yes.'

'Seb had to fight to get this one financed. He's wanted to do it for years. Since he left university. I remember him telling me about it then. He'll do anything to get it finished.' He paused. 'So she packs a lot of power, you see. Not only with the money, but she's also talented and sexy. And they tell me he can't keep his hands off her.'

He sounded so sceptical that Jo raised an enquiring eyebrow. Bill shrugged in answer.

'Oh, maybe. He likes women, though he doesn't let them get serious.'

They both looked across at Seb. While he was talking he had run his hands through his hair until it stood up in a peak. It made him look more like a fallen angel than ever. Jo felt an odd little clutch at her stomach.

He half turned, and a shock jolted through Jo, as if she had touched a live wire. It was ridiculous. At that distance it was not even possible for their eyes to meet. Yet it seemed as if he had, at least for a moment, locked on to her, and the whole force of his personality had lobbed her into shock.

She thought with a flash of recall of his mouth coming down on to hers; and the nightmare surfacing to swamp her. What was there about him that had this effect on her? As if, whenever he was in her sight, she was pulled towards him, willing or not. And she was not willing.

Beside her Bill said earnestly, 'I don't know what he's up to. But I don't think he's going to be exactly—er—impartial if someone has a row with Anna Beth Arden. Do you know what I mean?'

Jo tipped her head back and looked at the sky. 'A gypsy's warning?' she asked flippantly.

Bill dropped his voice. 'Don't make an enemy of her, Jo.'

Jo was watching Seb. 'And if she makes an enemy of me?'

'Keep your head down when you're together and out of her way whenever you can,' Bill said frankly. 'Seb's a good bloke, but if he's involved... Anyway, he's got to keep her sweet because of the backers. And if she's gunning for you...'

The message was unmistakable. Jo looked at him. He had an open face, currently creased with worry. Clearly, he did not relish talking about colleagues like this.

Jo said quietly, 'Why are you telling *me*? Did you warn off the others?'

'The others she ran out of town?' Bill said. He looked as if he found the subject distasteful. 'No. Only, I've seen the way she looks at you. And the way you don't look at her. You're not afraid of her, and she doesn't like it. And—you might be after Seb. So...' And he shrugged.

Jo jumped as if had struck her accidentally. She said harshly, 'There is no possibility of my being after Seb.'

Bill looked surprised at her tone. He said placatingly, 'As far as Anna Beth's concerned *any* woman might be after Seb.'

Behind them a deep voice Jo knew said in amusement, 'You flatter me. And exaggerate. I hope.'

Bill swung round. He was, Jo saw, quite unembarrassed. Unlike herself. She turned more slowly, carefully angling her gaze so that she looked at Seb's temple, and not into those dangerous dark eyes.

Bill said, grinning, 'She's had you staked out as private property from the day she arrived, Seb.'

Seb only responded with a shrug. He did not seem to care one way or the other. Jo wondered whether that was a sign of genuine indifference or part of the super-cool mask. She found she wanted to shake him. What would it take to disturb that lazy self-possession? Could Anna Beth do it? Could she, if she taunted him?

'Backer's rights?' Jo asked sweetly.

His reaction was not what she had hoped for. His eyes narrowed, but he laughed softly. 'An interesting thought.'

It was an obscure challenge. Jo felt the strength of his will beat at her as he tried to get her to meet his eyes. By a heroic feat of will of her own, she half turned away.

Bill seemed unaware of their silent battle. 'Rather you than me,' he was saying with a mock shiver. 'I'd as soon give the key of the door to a hungry shark.'

Seb's grin widened. 'That's because you're not used to ambitious women, Bill. You're just too old-fashioned.'

'Ambitious women don't have to eat you alive,' Bill objected, offended. 'Jo doesn't. And she's the most professional thing we've had here since we started.'

Seb flung back his head and laughed. 'Thank you!'

'Even you,' Bill said, unrepentant, 'dance around keeping people sweet. Jo just gets on with the job.'

'And the hell with everybody,' Seb agreed. There was a faint edge to his voice. He turned his gaze on her and said, thoughtfully, 'Have you ever tried to keep anyone sweet in your life?'

Jo was sufficiently startled to forget her policy of no confidences. It called up so many memories that she answered involuntarily, 'Not with any success.'

Seb's eyes narrowed again until they were almost slits. But before he could speak they were hailed by one of the technicians.

Seb swung round neatly. The man waved an arm.

'Ah. Good. They've done it. Are you ready to go, Bill?'

Bill nodded, hitching up his breeches and walking off in the direction of his horse.

Seb looked Jo up and down. 'You?'

She was suddenly very conscious of the fact that the rags that Sue and Lisa had rapidly contrived were very ragged indeed. She resisted an impulse to pull the front of the torn frills together, and looked at his temple again.

'Fine.'

He gave a short sigh. 'Yes, you bounce back quickly, don't you? It's hard to remember that a couple of hours ago you were passing out.' He looked at her searchingly. 'Do you know why?'

The shadow of the nightmare flickered, mocking her. Jo felt her breath shorten, and carefully steadied herself. But she knew he had registered that tell-tale tremor.

She shrugged, not answering.

'You were fine after the dive.' It was not a question. 'And you'd changed. So it wasn't suffocation, climbing the hill in all that velvet.' He paused. 'It was me, wasn't it?'

Jo's throat felt constricted. She shook her head. He did not believe her.

'*Why?*' Seb sounded baffled. 'I'm sorry I lost my temper. I thought you'd gone over accidentally. Maybe drowned. You must have realised. Anyway, you're not afraid of me...' He broke off abruptly.

Jo was not conscious of it, but she must have made some small movement. Seb stared at her, incredulous. Jo stared back.

'I don't believe it,' he said at last, flatly.

She moistened her dry lips.

'You're not afraid of anything. And you've been fighting with me since you arrived, so I don't see why another bout should make much difference,' he drawled.

'It didn't,' Jo said curtly.

Seb paid no attention to that. He looked intrigued. 'Because I shouted? Or because I kissed you?'

Jo swallowed. 'No,' she said in a strangled voice.

Seb took no notice of that either. 'Is that it?' He sounded thoughtful. 'OK, we were both a bit shaken. But hell, Jo, you've been kissed before.'

The nightmare was there, like a ghost that only she could see, fleeting and mocking, making her skin clammy and her hands shake. She looked past him, blinded by the demons.

'Only too often,' Jo said unwarily.

'*What?*'

Seb did not like that. She could see it, though she did not understand why.

Jo said hurriedly, 'I mean, I don't like to get involved with professional colleagues.'

There was a pause. Then Seb said quietly, 'That wasn't what you meant.'

There was another shout from behind them. Bill was mounted and his horse was prancing. With a low murmur, Jo turned to the tree and began to climb. Seb did not try to prevent her. But, as she reached the lower branches and glanced down, he looked up, straight into her eyes.

'You and I,' he said softly, 'are due a long, frank talk. Soon.'

And then he turned on his heel before she could think of anything to say.

*　　*　　*

They worked hard for a couple of hours. Simon was in evidence again, clearly happier when he was busy. Jo climbed and jumped out of the tree three times, her clothes getting progressively more torn. On the last shot, as she scrambled to her feet in front of Bill and his horse, the maltreated shirt collapsed, finally, to her waist.

Seb called, 'Cut.'

The cameras stopped whirring. Bill rode up to Jo and leaned forward with a pantomime leer.

'Going my way, honey?' he said, lifting her hat off, and chuckling. 'Wanna ride?'

There was a great shout of laughter. Jo grinned, hauling up the tattered remnants of her frills and holding them against her breast.

'I get horse-sick,' she told him gravely. 'But thanks for the offer.'

'You'd better not,' Seb remarked, coming up to them. 'You've got a lot of riding to do this week.' He looked at her and his eyes began to dance. 'How the hell did you get into that state?'

'Your heroine,' she informed him, 'has a tough life.'

He was unbuttoning his own shirt, grinning. 'I can't argue with that. Here, you'd better have this.' And he flung her the washed-out blue cotton he had been wearing.

Startled, Jo caught it, letting her rags fall as she flung out a hand to do so. Seb's grin widened.

'Put it on, my love. Before you get sunburn or the ravening wolf on the horse leaps on you.'

Bill was twirling her hat on one finger. He laughed. Jo thrust her arms into the shirt, trying not to notice that it was still warm from that vital body.

'OK,' she said resignedly. 'Laugh at me. You try climbing in and out of olive trees and see if you do any better. I told the wardrobe girls it was a wonder the character had any clothes left at all after the things you've given her to do.'

'Not me,' said Seb virtuously. 'The author. We are talking world literature here.'

Jo shut her eyes in despair. 'That is, of course, a comfort,' she said politely. 'When I get into that hot bath I keep dreaming about, I'll tell my bruises they were got in the cause of literature.'

'Do that,' said Seb. 'Whenever you like. I don't need you again today.'

Jo flexed her shoulders. 'Thank heavens,' she said devoutly.

Back at the house she made straight for her room. She was aching comprehensively. Although she fell as she had been trained to fall, light and relaxed, the earth was baked hard as concrete. That last time, though, she had caught her hip quite a nasty blow. Still, it was part of the job and she had had worse. Slowly she began climbing the stairs to the gallery.

Halfway up she stopped. Standing at the top of the flight, looking down at her, was Anna Beth Arden. Her face looked strange. Jo shook her head, puzzled.

Instantly the odd expression disappeared, and Anna Beth smiled down at her. 'Had enough?' she drawled, and as Jo raised her eyebrows added charmingly, 'You know, I do so admire you.'

Jo got to the top of the stairs. Anna Beth did not get out of her way. For a moment they stood there facing each other, the actress in a silk blouse and gold chains over softly flowing trousers that were cut to show every curve, Jo in jeans and Seb's shirt.

'Now that,' Jo said frankly, 'comes as a surprise.'

Anna Beth widened her eyes at her. 'Oh, no,' she assured her earnestly. 'I couldn't do what you do. I'd just get so tense, trying to be somebody else. Having to move like them. Stand like them. Why, you and I, we're not even the same—height.'

Jo received a waft of heavy perfume as Anna Beth touched her shoulder to her own.

'How can you really convince yourself you're me?' Anna Beth said, making her point with a cat-like smile.

Jo met her eyes squarely and stood up a little straighter. 'Familiarity,' she said levelly. 'I think I know you pretty well, Anna Beth. Don't forget I've worked with you before. It helps.'

The big brown eyes flickered. Then she was smiling again. 'I'm so glad,' she purred. 'I must tell Seb how very pleased I am that you're working for me.'

And, with a queenly inclination of the head, she went gracefully down into the courtyard.

Jo looked after her, her mouth dry. In that little exchange, she thought, the honours were just about even. Except that Anna Beth had had the last word, of course.

She spent twenty minutes in the bath soaking in scented water and telling herself she didn't mind Anna Beth having the last word. What she did mind—and was not going to put up with—was Simon's making a fool of her.

She cornered him before dinner. Simon looked faintly panic-stricken.

'Look,' she said crisply, 'it's no business of mine if you're the worst PA in the business. But I don't like being shouted at. And I don't like being made to look unprofessional. What was it all about?'

Simon went a dull red. 'I don't know what you mean,' he said sullenly.

Jo tapped her foot with impatience. 'You don't even *sound* convincing,' she told him. 'Come along, Simon. Give.'

'It's the backer,' he said at last, startling Jo into nearly dropping her glass of wine. 'It's because he's married to Anna Beth you see. He wants her to——' he flushed '—well, to do everything herself. He doesn't want her having to share the credits with anyone.'

Jo drank some wine and said carefully, 'And how does Anna Beth feel about this?'

But, on this, Simon was able to answer with shining innocence. 'Oh, she thinks he's crazy. She's terrified. She...' He went red again but this time, Jo thought, with the intensity of his feelings. 'She's going to leave him, you know. She's scared of him.'

Jo looked down at her glass. She considered and discarded a number of answers to that. But, if she was any judge, Simon was pretty far gone. He would believe what he wanted to believe. Just as her mother had done. Love, she thought, shivering a little, puts a bandage over your eyes and scrambles your brains.

She said gently, 'Why mess up my dive, Simon? What was it meant to achieve?'

Simon suddenly looked like a small boy who had been caught out. 'Because Seb *had* been saying that you were too much of a prima donna for your own good and he was going to sort you out,' Simon explained sunnily. 'If he thought you were souping things up to make them look more spectacular, he'd think it was to boost your own reputation.'

Thank you, Seb, thought Jo savagely. To say nothing of this retarded romantic who ought never to have been let out on his own.

'Then he'd fire you. You're his last chance to get the stunts done. So they'd have to get Chris to write a couple more scenes for Anna Beth after that.'

She stared at him, speechless. He seemed to believe it implicitly. Jo shook her head, feeling helpless. How naïve could you be?

'Anna Beth must have been impressed,' she said at last.

Simon shot her a sharp look. 'She doesn't know. It was my idea.'

I'll just bet it was, thought Jo. But it was clear he believed it. She said, 'Well, it didn't work. You mustn't try anything like it again, Simon. No matter how much you want to please—er—the backer. It's not worth it. If I'd been hurt, the company wouldn't have been properly insured. I would have said I had done it on instructions. Seb would have said I hadn't. You would have had to go to court and tell the truth—or lie on oath. And where would your career have gone after that?'

Simon looked horrified. 'But surely, it wasn't that dangerous?'

'Simon,' Jo said patiently, 'just about everything I'm doing on this film is dangerous. That's what Seb is paying me for, even if it hurts him. Because *I'm* taking the risks. Not your star. Me. And anything that's done to look like an accident is bound to be trickier than something properly approached, like that dive was supposed to be. What's more,' she added, to clinch it, 'if you do any-thing else that stupid, I'm going to get my agent to ask for a specific additional indemnity.'

Simon looked blank.

'And I shall tell him why,' Jo said on a gust of rage.

He was alarmed. 'But they'll think that Anna Beth...'

He came to that conclusion very quickly, Jo thought, if he really had thought the spiteful little scheme up all on his own. She lifted her shoulders in an indifferent gesture.

'That wouldn't be fair,' Simon said with dignity.

Jo remembered what the wardrobe girls had said about his chivalrous instincts, and sighed.

'Look,' she offered, 'you make sure there are no more accidents. And I mean *no more*, Simon. Not so much as hot coffee down my cleavage. And I won't say any more about it.'

He looked at her, plainly torn between affront and half-fearful hope.

'Brownie's honour,' Jo murmured.

Affront won.

'Do what you like,' Simon snapped. 'You've got no proof. I shall deny it if you say anything. Seb thinks you're a mischief-maker anyway. And he's right.'

He stalked away.

CHAPTER FIVE

JO WENT thoughtfully up to the gallery. At this hour of the evening a number of people were sitting along it, looking down into the courtyard where the staff were laying the long tables for dinner. There was a pleasant buzz of conversation.

Jo stopped for an instant, taking in the scene. The sounds of crockery and the smell of jasmine rose up from below her.

She went along the gallery to her own room. The double doors were open on to the gallery, as she had left them. Someone had been in to take away her clothes for washing and tidy up. They had also brought her some mail.

It was lying on the curlicued dressing-table, two forwarded from the flat, two directed to her here. Jo sighed and picked them over. A bill; a letter from her mother—never good news, that; one from Jerry; and one from her grandfather. The bill, she thought ruefully, was probably the best of the bunch.

She picked up the letters and her shoulder-bag, and took them outside. She pulled one of the basket chairs to the edge of the balustrade. A tumble of clematis and jasmine grew over it, shading the gallery heavily, so that she was hidden from most casual eyes. She slit open the first envelope.

The bill was easy: for repairs to the car. She had been expecting it. She dealt with it and turned reluctantly to the other three.

Jerry wanted her to do a film in Hungary as soon as she got back. He said it was all standard stuff, then added, not very encouragingly to Jo's mind, that she had done a period of circus training, hadn't she? The fee, though, was good. Jo took out her diary and pencilled in the dates. She would write to Jerry after dinner this evening.

Grandpa's letter was different. That was as bad as she could have feared. He did not say so, but it was obvious that he had given up hope.

It was just as well, thought Jo, that he had given her power of attorney, or he would already be signing over his beloved home to her father out of despair. At the thought of her father, her hands clenched. Hurriedly she straightened her fingers and turned to her mother's missive.

It was absolutely standard. It was even, Jo thought, funny if you didn't know what was behind it.

Cynthia had heard that Jo was encouraging the old man to be difficult about developing the Court. Of course, it was nothing to her what Alan did these days, but really, Jo should realise that money was men's *business*. John said if there was *anything* he could do Jo was to get in touch with him. She had his private number in London, didn't she? John was always *so* anxious to be a good stepfather and Jo had always been so *very difficult*. But if there was anything he could do now, he would be *delighted*.

Jo had destroyed her record of his private number in London when she was still at school. She was surprised he had told her mother he had given it to her. But then, Cynthia was adept at seeing only what she wanted to see. And she had quite definitely not wanted to see that her young husband—— Jo cut off the memory. There was no point in dwelling on it. She had dealt with it, and it was over. She crumpled Cynthia's letter viciously.

And Seb Corbel came round the trailing foliage and looked down at her.

'You look very fierce,' he said.

Jo jumped. She stared up at him. He had showered and changed, of course, so he no longer looked like the dusty adventurer who had given her his shirt; though she could remember a little too clearly how the tanned, smooth skin moved over the lithe frame. Her throat dried at the memory. Gritting her teeth, she braced herself as if for a challenge.

Seb watched her, frowning faintly. But all he said was, 'Our talk. I think now's as good a time as any, don't you?'

Jo looked away. She had not really expected to get out of it. Only, after her mother's letter and the sludge of memory it had stirred, she was not at her strongest. She straightened in her chair.

Seb sank into a chair beside her and stretched his long legs out in front of him. Below them people were gathering for dinner but, behind the jasmine, they were invisible. They might as well have been alone.

He said abruptly, 'Why did you pull that dive stunt?'

He looked more than ever like a fallen angel tonight, she thought suddenly. His face looked etched with a tiredness that was bone-deep, and his eyes were hooded. It was not a comfortable image. Her heart lurched when she thought of offering Simon up to Seb in this implacable mood. She said carefully, 'I thought it was what you wanted——'

But he interrupted. 'You knew damned well what I wanted. It was there in black and white. Wasn't it?'

She would have to keep her head if she wanted to deflect his anger. 'Yes, but——'

Seb swept on. 'Only you thought you knew better? Could get into the headlines with a death-defying leap?'

In spite of her resolution, Jo's anger began to simmer. She said coldly, 'I thought I was following your instructions.'

'Oh? We're in extra-sensory communication?' Seb asked. 'I've been sending you thought messages?'

Jo set her teeth. 'There's no need to be sarcastic.'

He said, 'Look, I'm the director. I've got to keep the balance between a lot of talented and temperamental people. I've got to stay impartial. I'm just trying to understand.'

She rounded on him. 'No, you're not. You're trying to be nasty. Heaven knows why. Maybe you just want to get your own back because I made you lose your cool for a moment.'

His eyes gleamed. He looked like a fallen angel who had been given the week's tally of sinners, Jo thought sourly.

'Well,' he drawled, 'if you did, it was mutual. Wasn't it?'

For a moment she did not understand. She had been talking about his alarm when he came pelting down the hill after her. But Seb was clearly thinking about the kiss. It seemed to have restored his good humour, too.

Jo felt her colour rise and fought furiously to hang on to her poise. She said icily, 'You startled me.'

Seb slanted a smile down at her. 'Mmm. I remember.'

This time she did not blush. She sent him a glare. 'I was not expecting to be jumped on. It was a shock.'

The sardonic smile grew. 'More of a shock than diving head-first into a mountain lake?' Seb sounded intrigued.

'Much,' Jo said crushingly.

'I knew it was exceptional,' he said in a satisfied tone.

Their eyes met, his lazily amused but somehow quite implacable. Jo thought longingly of hitting him and discarded the idea almost at once. She was fairly sure he would retaliate, notwithstanding the distant presence of their colleagues. She did not think Seb Corbel would find the thought of an audience much of a restraint.

She said faintly, 'I don't know what you're talking about.'

Suddenly he did not look amused any more. 'Maybe you don't, at that.' His eyes searched her face. 'Something happened out there, though. I want to know what it was. One minute you were kissing me—really kissing me—and the next...'

Jo's throat suddenly felt like sandpaper. She could remember, too vividly, the suffocating beat of his pulses, of her own, and the horrible menace of his laboured breathing.

'You're doing it again,' Seb said softly.

With an effort she brought her eyes to his face. She swallowed. 'What?'

'Looking scared to death.'

She drew in her breath in surprise. It sounded harsh.

'I don't like it,' Seb said conversationally.

Jo swallowed again. 'You're imagining it.'

His eyes were acute. 'No.'

'I'm not afraid,' she said proudly. 'It's not my style. I've worked for some horrors, and I'm not afraid of any of them. Certainly not of you.'

He was looking thoughtful. 'Maybe not me. Us?'

At the soft words, Jo felt suddenly as if the bottom had fallen out of her stomach. The lurch was almost physical. She grabbed the arms of her chair to steady herself. It was like being in a plunging lift.

'Don't look so appalled.' Seb sounded lazy, but he was still looking at her as if she were a specimen on which he was experimenting. 'I know Jerry said you don't like my reputation, but you've got to join the adult world some time.'

There was anger there, under the amusement.

'I don't know what you mean.'

'Don't you?' He hesitated. 'I've done a bit of background work on you, you know. You're costing us an arm and a leg, and I needed to know what sort of problems you were going to throw up.'

'And?' demanded Jo, seething. She held on to her anger. If she stayed angry she could ignore that stupid, superstitious feeling that somehow he had managed to dig out all the things she had buried—her father; Cynthia; the unwelcome affection of her stepfather.

'Not one.' He sounded almost angry. 'And no human relationships either.'

Jo winced. I am being punished, she thought. She set her teeth.

Watching her, he said quietly, 'What was it, Jo? A love-affair that went wrong?'

She concentrated on the tangled creeper in front of her and tried to ignore the insidious voice. She held her hands in her lap as still as stone.

'A bad marriage?'

In spite of herself, she made an involuntary movement. She stilled it at once but, without looking at him, she knew he had seen it and would store it up for future examination.

Seb said musingly, 'So that's it.'

Jo could not bear it. She said, with precision, 'I have never married. I never will.'

There was an electric silence. Below them someone started to play the guitar. It sounded sad, and yet somehow savagely angry; very much as she felt herself, Jo thought wryly. She looked up.

Seb was frowning. He too looked angry, she realised; shaken. But when he spoke he sounded no more than mildly interested. 'Never? Now, why?'

For no reason at all that she could think of, Jo told him. 'I'm the child of a marriage that shouldn't have happened,' she told him emptily. 'They paid for it. So did everyone else. My father is still...' She stopped, a pain stabbing across her brows. She put up a hand to it.

'Collecting his debts?' Seb offered after a pause.

Jo bit her lip. She did not need to answer. He was too clever, she thought, in despair.

'From you?'

With a great effort she dropped her hand from her eyes. She even shrugged. 'Partly. More from my grandfather. I suppose he thinks he should have made my mother keep on doing her duty, even though my father was playing around all over Europe.' Her voice was hard. A stranger would have thought she was quite indifferent. 'He's a powerful man, my father. My grandfather's old, and scared of him.'

She could feel Seb's eyes on her like a palpable touch. She kept her face cold.

'But not you?' Seb murmured. It sounded almost as if there was anger licking through the soft voice.

Jo could not understand it. She shrugged again. 'He makes a lot of noise. I grew up with it. And temper doesn't scare me.'

'Not a lot does,' agreed Seb neutrally. 'What did he threaten to do to your grandfather?'

'Turn him...' Jo began unwarily. She stopped.

'Turn him out,' deduced Seb.

'I'd prefer not to discuss it.'

He gave an unamused laugh. 'Another one for the list.'

Jo did look up then. His face was dark with anger.

'You don't want to talk about your family, your past...' He was ticking them off on his fingers. He gave her a mocking look. 'What happens when we touch...'

Jo flinched and her eyes fell. She became aware that her fingers were twisting and twisting in her lap, and knew he was watching them. She felt horribly exposed. She stiffened her spine and heard him laugh.

'My friend the android. Only you don't kiss like an android,' he said softly. 'At least not until you remember.'

Jo gasped. 'That's sexual harassment,' she choked when she could speak.

His eyebrows rose. 'Threatening a walk-out?' Seb drawled.

She was rather pleased with the reaction. At least she had deflected him from her private life. She said with composure, 'Only if you behave badly.'

His smile grew. It was not a particularly pleasant smile. Nor was it very encouraging to pick up the strong impression that he was enjoying the exchange.

'How badly?' Seb murmured with relish.

Jo glared. 'Any repeat of today's performance, and I quit.'

His eyes met hers. Locked. She straightened.

But in the end all he said was, 'Likewise.'

She was confused. 'What?'

'Any more unauthorised courting of risks, and you're out.' His voice was hard. 'With a Press statement to say why. Of course, if you don't care about publicity that won't bother you.'

'I care about my *skin*,' Jo said in exasperation. 'I'm not in the business of doing anything more dangerous than you're paying me to.'

His face set. It was clear that he did not believe a word. He had already made up his mind. She wondered who had helped him—Anna Beth?

'So much for the impartial director,' Jo mocked.

She thought she saw him wince at that one. But he was getting up, pushing back his chair and looking down at her with an expression that was neither lazy nor professionally indifferent.

'This was not quite the talk I had in mind,' he said. 'Still, it has been illuminating. And, when the movie is finished, you and I are going to get down to brass tacks, Jo Page.'

She did not understand him, but she understood that he was threatening her. She came to her feet in a bounce of anger.

'Oh, no, we're not. When the movie is finished, I'm never going to work for you again. Jerry can say what he likes. And you can multiply the salary by *ten* and you won't get me back.'

Seb's eyes glinted. 'One day I'll make you take that back.'

She nearly didn't go down to dinner that night. She was, she assured herself, much too angry to meet Seb with civility.

But in the end hunger got the better of her. The first thing she saw was Anna Beth wrapped round Seb at the end of one table. Anna Beth pointedly ignored her. Seb was looking more than usually absent-minded, making notes on a dog-eared script. He did not look up. Miguel, however, saw her and waved.

'Ready for tomorrow?' he asked cheerfully, jumping to his feet as she threaded her way through the casually placed chairs. 'I must say, you look very fit. I'd be flat on my back under a sun-lamp if I'd done what you have today.'

Jo immediately felt better. His uncomplicated friend-liness was a tonic. She grinned, and sat down in the chair he held for her.

'Do you know Carlos Andrade?' Miguel asked, in-troducing the man on his other side.

Jo leaned forwards to shake hands, interested. The Olympic fencer was a neat, small-boned man, but she could feel the strength in the firm handshake.

He said, 'I have never worked in films before, but I have been hearing about you, Miss Page.'

'Jo, please.' She looked at him with undisguised mis-giving. 'Er—what have you been hearing about me?'

He gave a smile that was a blinding flash of perfect teeth. 'That you terrified my friend Seb out of his di-rector's chair today, for one thing.'

Miguel said apologetically, 'Everyone's talking about it, Jo. Our super-cool director just doesn't behave like that.'

Jo sighed. 'Maybe that was why he was so angry.'

Miguel looked curious. 'Angry?' He sounded disbelieving.

'From where I stood,' Jo said firmly, 'it looked as if he was as mad as he could get.'

He looked quizzical. But all he said was, 'Well, it was a wonderful shot anyway. And there's lots more to do now, so we can all forget about it.'

But he was too optimistic. The whole crew was talking about Seb's memorable behaviour; with, Jo discovered, one or two embellishments. It had not escaped notice that he had given her his shirt that afternoon. And they were all watching Anna Beth.

Anna Beth, though, was being particularly charming.

'Honey,' she said the next day, when they were on the hill together, 'don't let Seb get to you. He plays games.'

Jo curbed her dislike. 'Thanks for the warning,' she said drily.

'He and I go *way* back,' Anna Beth told her in a throaty drawl. 'And when he's working he can be a devil. I know. He just doesn't notice, poor darling.'

'Oh, I'd say he knew,' Jo said.

'He's so wrapped up in the movie, he doesn't think about people,' Anna Beth confided. 'He'll be sorry later.'

Jo gave her a level look. 'Sorry for what?'

Anna Beth shook the red curls reproachfully. 'Honey, you don't have to pretend. He *told* me. We don't have secrets.'

Jo raised one eyebrow but did not otherwise answer. It made Anna Beth lose some of her sweetness.

'Look, the guy's dynamite. You know it. I know it. Seb'll do anything for his movie. But he never gets serious.'

'Oh, I'm sorry to hear that,' Jo said with spurious sympathy.

The last of Anna Beth's sweet understanding went with a pop. 'Don't get any ideas, that's all. Seb Corbel is a man who knows where he's going. And a little nobody of a stunt girl isn't going to get in his way.'

Or, Jo thought, yours. But she was not unwise enough to say it. She had indulged herself sufficiently for one day, she thought.

Even so, Anna Beth made her pay for it. Jo was supposed to be watching the filming of Anna Beth's scene so that, when she did the riding in the immediately subsequent shot, she could catch the same mood.

But Anna Beth wasn't projecting any mood at all. She was, quite simply, furious, and she was not going to cooperate with anyone until her temper had worked itself out. They shot the take over and over again, while Anna Beth forgot her words, forgot to move, and eventually looked into the face of the man playing her father and said, 'Stop staring at me like that.'

'Cut,' said Seb. He said it very quietly but there was not much doubt about his feelings.

He went over to the actors. 'What is the problem?'

Neither of the two men involved answered. Anna Beth swung round, her curls dancing on the shoulders of her brocade jacket. The big eyes were swimming. 'Oh, Seb, it's so *mean*.'

He did not shout as he had done at Jo. He took the little hands with great gentleness between his own, and said in a coaxing tone that Jo would not have recognised, 'What's the matter, sweetheart?'

'This scene. It's so important. It's so *me*. I'm putting *everything* into it. And then you won't let me finish it.'

Lisa, who was standing with Jo watching this performance, murmured in her ear, 'Daddy has the finest stable in the South, according to her, and she's been riding since she was an embryo.'

Anna Beth was now drooping towards Seb. Lisa snorted.

'Darling, you might just as well put a sack of potatoes in my clothes and put it on top of that horse. She's not an actress. She doesn't *feel* the way I do.'

That, understandably, got a snigger. Even Jo, who determined to take no part in the scene, found that she had to cough hard to suppress her amusement. None of that, of course, put Anna Beth in any sweeter a temper.

'Nobody,' declared Anna Beth tragically, 'understands what it does to me to see some *gymnast* destroying the character I've lived with so long.'

That was not quite so funny. Nobody laughed.

In Jo's ear Lisa said, 'Bitch.' She sounded gloomy but unsurprised.

Seb was saying soothingly that he did understand, really he did; that Anna Beth, like all great artists, was too close to her work and wasn't able to judge properly.

'As long as he doesn't tell her what he was telling the others last night,' Lisa murmured. 'Apparently, the stunts are bloody marvellous. If he tells her that, she'll kill him.'

Jo nodded. 'Or me.'

She watched the little scene impassively. Anna Beth was now curled confidingly against him. 'It *hurts* me,' she was saying plaintively.

'And it's because we don't want you to be hurt that we're asking someone else to do these things,' Seb said with inspired patience. 'They're not very important, after all. You're too precious to risk, you know.'

'Clever,' said Lisa approvingly.

'He manipulates well,' Jo agreed, and earned herself a sharp look. 'Still, he's got a film to finish. Hang on: it looks as if we're off again.'

And, sure enough, after a murmured exchange, Seb and Anna Beth parted and went to take up their positions ready for another take. Anna Beth sailed through it. And the next. And the next.

Passing Jo after the last take of the morning, she said, 'Are you getting the idea?'

It could have been kindly meant. They both knew it wasn't.

Jo said, straight-faced, 'Yes, I think I can see what you're after.'

For a moment the melting brown eyes were as hard as pebbles. Then Anna Beth said in a purring voice, 'I'm so glad. It's *so* important we understand each other.'

'I couldn't,' said Jo fervently, 'agree more.'

There was a pregnant pause. Then the other girl turned on her heel. Jo looked after her thoughtfully.

'Amusing,' said a voice behind her. 'But inflammatory.'

Jo turned. Seb's face was unusually grim. He had been patience itself so far today, but he was looking tired, she saw. And his mouth was compressed in a tight line as if he was holding himself in check with a great effort.

'I'd be grateful,' he said curtly, 'if you could keep your mouth shut if you haven't anything useful to say.'

There was a thunderous silence. Miguel and Simon, who were coming up to join them, stopped dead. A cold fury took hold of her. She coolly looked him up and down. 'Temper,' she reminded him softly, 'doesn't frighten me.'

Their eyes clashed. Then Seb gave her a look of disgust and strode off.

Miguel whistled. 'You like to live dangerously, don't you?'

Jo lifted one shoulder, irritated. 'He annoys me.'

'He does more than that.' Miguel looked at her, his expression one of unholy amusement. 'You should see yourselves.'

Jo felt uneasy, but before she could demand an explanation, Simon, ignoring the whole scene, said earnestly, 'Anna Beth isn't like that underneath, you know.'

Miguel, looking amused, excused himself. Jo pushed up the cuffs of her shirt with exasperation. 'How far underneath?' she asked drily.

But Simon did not notice that either. He was obsessed with his goddess, Jo thought, reluctantly sorry for him.

'No. Really. You don't understand. She just has to do what her husband tells her.' Jo did not say anything, but she must have looked sceptical to Simon because he burst out, 'It's not fair. Everyone's against her. And she's only a child. They're all giving her orders and playing on her feelings until she doesn't know what she's doing.'

Jo refrained from saying that it looked to her as if Anna Beth knew very well what she was doing; or that she was playing pretty successfully on Simon's feelings. Instead she slipped an arm through his and said, 'It's a claustrophobic atmosphere, being on location. Everything looks different when you get back home. Let's go and find a breeze and talk about home.'

He was placated. He was, thought Jo ruefully, only too easy to placate. Anna Beth was not going to have much difficulty keeping her image intact with Simon. She sighed. It did not bode well for any future pranks that Anna Beth might have in mind.

They went and sat under an apricot tree. Jo leaned back against its knobbly bark with a sigh of contentment. 'It's so peaceful here.'

Simon lowered himself to the grass and turned over on his stomach. He too sighed. 'We were lucky to get it. It's very much a family home, you know, in spite of its history.'

Jo thought about it; then gave a nod. 'Yes, it feels like a family house.' She thought some more, and then grinned. 'A nice family.'

Simon gave a short laugh. 'I can't remember our home when the parents weren't fighting,' he said suddenly. 'Fighting and winning prizes. Heaven knows how they got themselves a son like me. I couldn't even get a job without my uncle finding it for me.'

Jo's heart twisted with compassion. But she knew it would be fatal to show it. So instead she said calmly, 'Your uncle isn't keeping it though, is he?'

Simon gave a short, surprised bark of laughter. 'You have a point,' he admitted. 'Though the way things are going...' He stopped. For a moment he stared upwards, frowning. Then he turned on his elbow, looking up into her face. He plucked a long strand of grass and began to stroke it thoughtfully down his face. 'What about you? Proud parents boasting of your success to the neighbours?'

It was so different from reality that Jo laughed aloud.

Simon's interest quickened. 'Not proud of you?' he said, sounding incredulous.

Jo smiled at him. 'They're terrified I'll get them into the papers,' she said frankly. 'My father is—well, a mega-entrepreneur is the best way of describing him. The Press don't like him, and the theory is that if I get picked up for drug-smuggling or running off with a film star's husband, they'll use it to get at him.'

Simon looked fascinated. 'Have you...? No.'

'No,' Jo agreed, amused. 'But I *could*.' She frowned heavily and imitated her mother's ladylike tones. '*Darling*, you know what film people are *like*.'

'And they both think like that?' He sounded disbelieving.

'Well, they always seem as bad as each other,' Jo said fairly, 'but they're probably not. My mother minds because she remarried some time ago and keeps hoping that people will forget about her first marriage. My father...' Her voice hardened a little. 'Well, my father doesn't really care about anything very much, except where the next million is coming from.'

She remembered where his next million was likely to come from and looked grim.

Simon said slowly, 'Do you—get on badly?'

'I never see him,' Jo said with simple truth. 'I don't hate him or anything like that. Although I get quite close to it when he tries to throw my grandfather on to the streets...' She bit it off, but too late.

Simon sat bolt upright, an almost comical expression of fascination on his face. This was clearly a story of a dimension to take his mind off his own troubles. Jo could have kicked herself.

But, having said so much, there was no way she could back down now. 'My grandfather lives in an old house. Nothing like this, of course, but he bought it when he was younger and it's rather pretty with quite a lot of land. By a river. He—loves it. I spent a lot of time there after the divorce.'

When she was running away from both parents, who did not want her, and the stepfather who perhaps wanted her a little too much. Though at thirteen she had not quite seen it like that. She had just been unhappy, and desperately grateful for the haven in the ramshackle house. It was not until this year that she had found that Grandpa had had to mortgage it; and that her father had acquired the mortgage.

'My father thinks that my grandfather should go into sheltered housing. And that the house and grounds should be developed; time-share flats in rural England. There's a lot of money in time-share, according to my father.'

'He sounds a tough nut,' Simon said blankly.

'He doesn't let sentiment get in the way of business,' Jo agreed.

'Will he get away with it?'

'Over my dead body,' said Jo grimly. She thought for a moment and then gave another laugh. 'Could be literally, if things carry on going the way they have been.'

Simon flushed and looked away.

'Don't say things like that,' a voice behind them said. 'Not even as a joke.'

They both jumped. Simon leapt to his feet.

Jo thought, confusedly, I didn't know he was there. I didn't pick him up on my sensors this time. I must be getting over it. And then thought—with a little jolt of shock—over *what*?

Seb ignored Simon. He strolled forwards and hunkered down beside her on the grass. Jo moved back a little by pure instinct. He gave her an unreadable glance.

'It's bad luck,' he said lightly. But his eyes were not laughing.

And, as if Simon were not there, he stretched out a long-fingered hand and ran the back of it down her cheek until she trembled.

CHAPTER SIX

IT WAS not, of course, a sensible thing for Seb to do. Unless, thought Jo viciously, he was positively seeking gossip. Simon's eyes grew as round as gob-stoppers and he looked distinctly uncomfortable.

Seb, apparently oblivious, smiled warmly down into Jo's eyes.

She took his hand, detached it from her cheek and handed it back to him, firmly. 'I don't believe in luck,' she said.

Not a whit bothered, Seb grinned. 'I do. Especially the luck I make myself.'

Simon said curiously, 'Seb, do you really think there's a jinx on this movie?'

Seb turned to him lazily. Jo thought she caught the flash of steel in his eyes, but he was smiling as he shrugged. 'Do you?'

Simon did not seem to know what to say. Seb waited for an answer. When it did not come, he turned back to Jo. 'Maybe one or two people have let their egos get out of hand,' he murmured, quite as if he didn't care.

He was looking at Jo's hair. He might just as well have been stroking it, she thought, shivering.

Jo said quietly, 'Accidents aren't usually the result of damaged egos.'

Seb's mouth tightened, but Simon took the point up eagerly.

'No. That's true. It must be coincidence.'

'There's a lot that can go wrong on any film,' Seb agreed. 'And on this one, more than most, given what

99

we've written in as stunts. Maybe it's not so surprising, at that.'

He sounded infinitely weary all of a sudden. Jo had an almost overwhelming urge to touch the back of the hand lying on the grass so close to her thigh. She suppressed it. Had she not just told herself that, whatever it was that had formed this unexpected bond between her and Seb, she was getting over it?

But all she said was, 'If you're paying enough attention to safety and rehearsing properly, there shouldn't be any problem with stunts. It's when people start to cut corners that the problems start.'

Seb sighed. 'Well, we haven't cut any corners so far...'

Jo felt a shiver which had nothing to do with sexual attraction. If Seb Corbel was going to skimp rehearsal time, or something like that, it would give Anna Beth an appallingly easy opportunity for mischief.

She said sharply, 'You aren't going to start now?'

He didn't answer just at once. When he did it was to say in an odd voice, 'We've overshot. We're getting to danger point on the budget. I can't have this labelled the most expensive flop of the decade. And that's what it will be if I don't get it in the can soon.'

He was watching Simon narrowly. Simon frowned. 'It might be expensive. But why should it be a flop?'

'Because I'll have to cut the remaining scenes to the bone if I'm going to bring it in. Even in injury time,' Seb said. 'At least, I will if it goes on like this. It took us the whole morning to do one scene, today.'

He pushed his hand through his hair, making him somehow look younger and less horridly in charge of things, Jo thought.

Simon was saying excusingly, 'Anna Beth was out of sorts. She hasn't been well. You know that. She should have had a rest from filming...'

Jo had a sudden vision of the girl she had seen dancing up the staircase with her vibrant gypsy companion. She had not looked the wilting flower Simon was describing. She wondered sharply whether Seb knew about the gypsy. And whether he cared.

'Well,' Seb was saying, 'if this goes on there'll have to be a rewrite that takes her out of the remaining scenes altogether.'

Simon looked horrified. 'You can't do that. She's the main character.'

'I'd be reluctant to do that,' Seb told him equably. 'But Dona Luisa is only one of the main characters. I could shift the focus in Fernando's direction. If I had to.'

Simon said positively, 'It would mess up the film.'

Seb shrugged. 'Who knows? Sometimes the things you're forced into turn out surprisingly well.'

Simon scrambled to his feet. 'Not this.'

Another shrug. 'Let's hope we don't have to find out.' He looked up at Simon. 'Are you off?'

For no reason at all that Jo could see, Simon flushed. 'Tomorrow's running order. I'll let you have a revised list,' he muttered. 'You'll want it before tea.'

'I wanted it before lunch,' Seb murmured, watching Simon's departure with an unreadable expression. 'After this morning, I need all the running information I can get.'

Jo said to his averted profile, 'Are you serious about the rewrite? Wouldn't it spoil the film?'

Seb gave a sharp sigh. He said impatiently, 'Well, it wouldn't improve it.'

Jo watched him. 'But if you've spent so much already...'

He turned his head. 'Have you ever heard the one about throwing good money after bad? That's what the backers are going to be asking me quite soon.'

'But I thought . . .' Jo stopped abruptly.

Seb's face sharpened. 'You thought our star had a hand in the backing herself? Or at least her devoted husband did? Well, you were right. And it's more of a liability than you can imagine. And, however devoted he is, he didn't put up his millions to make a home-movie for the neighbours. He wants to see box office. And, frankly, so do I.'

It occurred to Jo suddenly that he was breaking all the rules by telling her this. It was the director's job to keep everyone sanguine, backers and performers alike. It did nobody any good if people started to get nervous about where their pay-packet was coming from.

She said slowly, 'Why are you telling me this?'

Seb tipped his head back. 'I'm not quite sure,' he said, disarming her. 'Maybe I feel I need someone on my side.' He gave her a long, unreadable look. 'Maybe I need you on my side.'

Jo drew a long breath. He was so close that she could see the tiny laughter lines round his eyes. In the hot air, his body generated even more heat. She felt surrounded by it; scorched by it. Trapped.

Over it? She faced the vividly unwelcome fact that whatever it was she felt for Seb Corbel she had only just begun to recognise the power of it.

His eyes grew intent.

In a familiar rhythm, her heart began to drum. In the recesses of her mind, the nightmare swirled. She swallowed.

Seb said quietly, 'It's happening again.'

Jo lifted her eyes to his, not understanding.

'What is there about me that makes you look like that?' he said in a musing voice.

Jo moistened her lips. 'Like what?'

'Don't tell me I'm imagining it,' he said curtly. 'If I touched you now you'd pass out on me again. Wouldn't you?'

The dark eyes were hard. Jo searched them. Seb Corbel did not like the way she reacted to him and he was not disguising it.

She looked away, her breathing rapid.

'*Wouldn't* you?'

Jo swallowed. 'Probably,' she said.

He did not touch her. She could feel him willing her to turn back and meet his eyes, but he did not lay a finger on her.

'You're going to have to get over that.'

Even then she did not look at him. 'I don't see that it matters,' she said with an effort. Out of the corner of her eye, she felt the strong body make a small movement, almost as if he had flinched.

'Maybe not to you,' he said at last. She had the feeling it was not what he had intended to say.

She kept her eyes on the prickly grasses around them. 'Or to you. Except in a very temporary way.'

Seb said very softly, 'If that's a challenge, I accept.'

There was silence. The whole world seemed to hold its breath. More than anything she had ever known, she wanted to reach out to the man at her side. Jo thought, frantically, What is *happening* to me? But all she said was, 'I don't understand.'

Seb laughed, and leapt lightly to his feet. He stood looking down at her, his expression mocking. 'Think about it,' he advised.

And was gone.

Jo did not have time to think about that disturbing remark, however. Immediately after he had left, a diminutive dispatch rider arrived with a revised running schedule, and Jo found in amazement that she was to rehearse and perform all her remaining scenes in the next five days. It was an inhuman demand. Most people would have refused to do it. But Jo, sensing an implied challenge, was put on her mettle. If Seb Corbel could do it, so could she.

And Seb himself seemed tireless. While the actors sweated and the technicians wilted, Seb stayed lazy and imperturbable. His tall figure seemed to be everywhere, though he never moved faster than his customary stroll. He seemed to have his finger on every pulse. And yet his clipboard was frequently abandoned on his unused canvas chair.

'He carries it all in his head,' Simon said, half envious, half admiring. 'It makes me feel surplus to requirements.'

'He'll have a revolution on his hands if he goes on like this,' Miguel said, not at all admiring. 'Bill was exhausted yesterday. He didn't even have any supper. Just went to bed.'

'This is not normal, then?' asked Carlos Andrade. The Olympic fencer was clearly fascinated and more than a little amused by the feverish activity.

Miguel shook his head. 'That's what the unions are for,' he said darkly.

But no one complained. And Jo was not the only one ready, dressed and be-wigged, at first light when Seb strolled out from his conference with the technicians.

She thought sometimes that there was an ironic light in his eyes when he saw her. But he was as grave as a judge when he directed her. Not polite, Jo thought wryly. No one could accuse him of treating her with kid gloves the way he did Anna Beth Arden. When things did not go the way he wanted, he could be caustic. Jo was no more immune from his sarcasm than any of the others. But he was impeccably grave. There was not so much as a hint of that teasing challenge that so disconcerted her. She missed it, though she would not have admitted it to him; she barely admitted it to herself.

On the day of the big riding sequence, Jo took her amiable horse out before filming started. She curtailed her run to do so. The stable-boy was sleepy but co-operative and the horse seemed pleased with the unexpected early exercise.

She went out along the cliff where she had made her disputed dive.

Jo looked down the inhospitable hill-face to the lake, now glinting like a diamond in the early sun. She shivered. She was still not sure whether Seb had accepted her version of the incident. He had never asked her who had told her to vary the stunt. She suspected that that was because he knew. But it might mean instead that he had simply decided to forget all about it. She had certainly had no indication that he had ever taken it up with Simon.

And as for Anna Beth, he was positively devoted, as far as one could see. Even Carlos Andrade, the newcomer, had commented on it. Anna Beth went everywhere with him. She stuck close all day during filming, to the supreme annoyance of the other actors. And in the house, in the evenings, she was at his side the entire time.

The gypsy did not reappear. Jo thought idly that she found that surprising. He had not had the look of one who would be easily got rid of—or put on hold. All that fierce life had made even Jo feel singed as she had watched from the shadows. What on earth must it have done for Anna Beth? And what game was she playing?

Jo turned the horse's head gently to the towering mountains. The beast clopped obediently over the stony ground. Jo thought of the exchange she had overheard at dinner last night. There was no doubt at all that she had been meant to overhear...

'Honey, you're just being stubborn,' Anna Beth said, caressingly, to Seb.

The girl was, thought Jo, with what she assured herself was wry detachment, only technically sitting on her own chair. She was curved seductively towards Seb's body, leaning both arms along his shoulder, her beautiful face tipped up to look at him. The melting brown eyes never left his mouth.

Seb seemed amused but not unappreciative. 'It's for your own good.'

'How *can* it be?'

'You're too precious to risk,' he said with great patience but considerable firmness.

Anna Beth wrinkled her nose and stretched up at him making a little kissing noise. 'I'm risking my reputation.'

Seb cocked an eyebrow at her. 'And I'm not?'

She punched him playfully on the jaw with a small fist. 'You know what I mean.'

He flicked her nose with a forefinger, not answering. Anna Beth gave a little wriggle and touched her lips to his jaw. Jo looked away. But she could not avert her eyes from the husky murmur that reached her.

'The scene is so important. The *key*. I want the audience to feel all the drama, the pathos... I want to show the *pain*...'

'That,' said Seb drily, 'is exactly what I'm afraid of. The answer is no.'

But Anna Beth was a trier, Jo acknowledged.

She wailed, 'But I can't bear to watch the way that woman murders it.'

'Then don't watch,' Seb said calmly.

'But——'

'Look, pet, this is not for negotiation. We've got a highly expensive expert. She does the stunts.' His voice softened. 'Why don't you just put it out of your mind? Go and see some sights. Dance at the fiesta. Go to Seville and buy yourself one of those dresses with the frilly skirts. Or take off to the coast and swim.'

There was a pause. Anna Beth stopped looking kittenish for a moment. Seb was unmoved. It was clear that she was not used to being denied.

Then she gave a charming shrug and moved back. She did not exactly withdraw her arm, thought Jo. She trailed her hand slowly along the bone of his shoulder, the arm socket and then down to his hand. There she twined her fingers through his and took his hand to her lips.

'You're very unkind,' she mourned.

Seb smiled at her. 'I'm very protective,' he corrected.

Jo shivered. She knew those soft tones only too well. She wondered if they had the same effect on Anna Beth as they did on her. It was not a comfortable thought.

But the other girl gave no sign of the quivering surrender that might have been expected. Instead she batted silken eyelashes and drawled, 'All right. Tell me about the fiesta.'

Seb looked round. 'Miguel's the guy to help you there. He heard about it when he went to Santa Ana yesterday.'

And they started to talk about important things like evening excursions and where the best vineyards in the area were.

*　　*　　*

Now, Jo sat on her horse and looked a little blindly over the intimidating landscape. That conversation had hurt her, oddly. She had seen Seb using the same technique on Anna Beth Arden as he did on her. Of course, the actress was more sophisticated, more sure of her own powers; she did not fall apart at the touch of his hand or the caressing note in his voice. But basically the technique was the same.

He sounded warm, but really the whole performance was a cold-blooded attempt to get you to do what he wanted, Jo thought. She winced, remembering how easily she had melted, how willingly she had fallen into the crazy workload he had decreed.

Oh, he was a brilliant director, Seb Corbel, no question. Harnessing all those talents and moulding them—working them like slaves—and all without even *trying* very hard. It was particularly humiliating that he had not had to try.

I was more than halfway to falling in love with him, Jo thought soberly. It would have been all too easy. Even though I know that type of professional Don Juan, and don't like it, I could *still* have fallen for him. She congratulated herself on avoiding the trap.

The horse began to sidle sideways, and Jo looked down to see in surprise how tightly she was clutching the reins. She released them at once. Presumably the animal had picked up her internal agitation.

She bent forwards and patted his neck. 'All right, old boy. I'm sorry. We'll go back now. Don't you start throwing a temper. You and me,' she told him solemnly, 'we're going to need each other today.'

But when she got back it was to a confused stable and a house in uproar.

Anna Beth was missing. So was a horse. They had no idea where either of them had gone.

'But presumably,' said Miguel grimly, 'they went together.'

Carlos Andrade, who had been running, was in the courtyard, a small towel slung round his neck. Despite his exertion, he looked cool and unflustered. He was the only person who did.

'But why?' he asked, puzzled. 'Surely nobody would have minded if she had wanted to ride? Why do it in secret?'

Miguel flashed an embarrassed look at Jo.

She said coolly, 'Anna Beth is convinced she could do the stunts better than I can.'

Andrade looked stunned. He had read the script. '*All* the stunts?' he echoed faintly.

Jo shrugged. 'Probably. Certainly the riding. She's been trying to persuade Seb Corbel. Now, presumably, she's taken off on horseback to prove her point.'

'Then she'll be out of luck,' Miguel said with undisguised satisfaction. 'Seb will have the whole scene in the can before she gets back.'

Jo felt an odd flicker of foreboding. 'I certainly hope so,' she said.

And at first it seemed as if her hopes were to be realised. The day was sharp and clear. Seb found the camera angles he wanted with miraculous ease. Jo and her friendly mount went through their paces twice, three times.

'That'll do,' Seb said briskly. He turned to the first unit cameraman. 'Keep the camera running until she is right in front of the coach. I know we've got another take scheduled. But it may not be necessary.'

The man, busy with his viewfinder, nodded.

Seb picked up his field telephone and said the same thing to the second unit. They were a mile away up the bare hillside. Jo was to start her ride from above and behind them, tracked by a unit on a Land Rover.

'Expensive,' Bill had commented when he saw the screen directions.

'Seb's not cutting any corners,' Simon had said proudly.

Bill had laughed. 'Not on the machinery, maybe.'

'Nor on the cast.'

Bill had sighed exaggeratedly. 'I know, I know. He bought the best. And he's certainly getting his money's worth out of us,' he'd added.

Now Bill was looking very handsome in a ruffled cotton shirt and riding breeches. The wardrobe girls had relented and allowed him out of his velvet jacket when Seb had agreed.

'Not before time,' he said. 'I was turning to butter in all that velvet.' He looked down at Jo and made a face at the red wig. 'How're you doing in all that horsehair?'

'Melting nicely,' she acknowledged. 'I must say, slave-driver or not, I'm with Seb on getting this damned scene over with as soon as possible.'

'Like before high noon,' Bill agreed with one eye on the blinding sky.

Seb strolled over. 'Ready?'

Jo nodded.

'Get moving, then. I'll talk to the Land Rover. It's already up there. But give me a wave when you're ready to start.'

She touched the red scarf at her throat. 'With this?'

'Don't go messing up the costume. Just fling your arms about,' Seb besought her. 'I'll see.' And he touched his binoculars.

'OK.' She vaulted lightly into the saddle and gave him a brisk smile. She nodded to Bill. 'See you at the stagecoach,' she said out of the corner of her mouth, and rode off with a wave.

It was an easy ride, uphill but gentle. She took the horse at little more than walking pace. He had to be fresh for the headlong gallop later. And anyway, it was too hot to go faster than one had to.

The horse was stepping delicately over a tiny creek when she heard a cry. At first she thought she had imagined it, but the horse's ears twitched too. He became uncharacteristically restless. Firmly Jo pointed his nose up the hill and urged him on. It was no good.

At last she let him go where he wanted to. He moved under some trees and behind a low stone wall. There, on the ground, was Anna Beth.

'Oh, heavens,' said Jo, cursing the fact that she carried no means of communication. She looked over her shoulder, but the main crew—all the crew—was out of sight, hidden by the wall and the trees. She rode up to the fallen girl.

'What happened?'

Anna Beth looked very pale. Her lovely hair had come undone in the fall and was tumbled all round her shoulders like Jo's infuriating wig.

She said with a catch in her voice, 'I've hurt my leg.'

'How?' said Jo, sliding to the ground.

The horse stood still enough, but he was tossing his head and stamping. Jo was surprised, but the important thing was not equine behaviour but how to get Anna Beth back to civilisation.

'I got off. I wanted a drink.' She indicated the little stream. 'I was crossing it and my leg—just seemed to give out.'

Her eyes were full of tears. She was obviously more shaken than one might have expected, thought Jo, trying hard to be sympathetic. She went down on one knee in front of the girl. 'Can you stand?'

'I—don't know. I couldn't earlier.'

'Try,' Jo suggested, offering her a shoulder.

Anna Beth put a small hand out and hauled herself up. She was breathing hard. She must be in pain, Jo thought, ashamed of herself.

The girl leaned back against the wall. Her hair was brilliant in the sunlight. She reached out a trembling hand to pat the nose of Jo's horse, as if looking for re-assurance from the animal. Her breasts rose and fell rapidly under the white shirt that was a copy of Jo's.

Jo thought suddenly, She doesn't look shaken; she looks *excited*.

What sort of game was she playing now?

But all Anna Beth did was to say, in a meek little voice, 'I'm so dry. Do you think you could...?'

'Fetch you some water?' Jo grinned at the cliché. 'OK, but it'll have to be in my hands. I've got nothing to carry it in.'

Anna Beth gave her a pathetically grateful smile. Jo turned back to the stream. Then she saw the reason that her horse was so restless. Anna Beth's mount was still there, standing under the shadow of the tree, pawing the earth.

Jo turned to say, 'Your horse didn't wander off, then,' and saw, too late, Anna Beth whisking herself into the saddle.

She wasted no words on questions or exclamations. As soon as she realised what was happening, she launched herself at the girl on the horse.

She nearly caught them too. Obviously Anna Beth in-tended to take the other horse with her, leaving Jo to make her way down the hill on foot. The actress made a grab for the loose reins but, as Jo lunged for her foot, she had to swerve away.

She took the horse just out of range, laughing. The excitement, the pleasure in her own cleverness, was now obvious. The beautiful mouth had taken on a slightly cruel line.

'Go and explain to Seb how you fell off your horse!' Anna Beth called breathlessly.

Jo measured the distance between them. She calculated that she could probably get Anna Beth off the horse with a flying leap. But it could be dangerous. The placid horse was patently disturbed. He was pulling at the reins and snorting. And Anna Beth, for all her proclaimed skill, was sliding around in the saddle. If she got the girl off the horse, she might also get the pair of them thoroughly kicked by the frightened animal, Jo realised with a sinking feeling.

So she tried reason. 'What are you trying to prove, Anna Beth?' she asked quietly.

The girl's laugh had the edge of hysteria. She did not answer directly. 'This is *my* part. *My* film. Nobody's going to push me out of my own film.'

'You're crazy,' Jo said wearily.

That seemed to catch her on the raw.

'And *you're* out of a job,' Anna Beth spat. 'I mean it.'

'I'm sure you do.' Once again, Jo spoke soothingly, taking a small step towards her.

At once the horse began to shake his head and snort. Anna Beth must have hauled, inadvisedly, on the reins.

'Keep away!' she said shrilly.

The horse did not like that either. He was stepping uneasily, turning this way and that. At the high-pitched protest, he seemed to make up his mind.

There was nothing Jo could do as the horse plunged round. Anna Beth was obviously taken by surprise. She lurched in the saddle and lost a stirrup. For a moment, Jo thought she was going to come off without any assistance from her. But then the horse turned again, sending Anna Beth lurching in the other direction, and, without more ado, took off down the hill.

Jo had a last glimpse of Anna Beth's white face and screaming mouth and he was among the trees and out of sight.

Her shoulders sagged. Seb, she realised, would be furious at this latest hold-up. And not without reason. He would not be very pleased with her for being so stupid as to get off her horse, either.

She sat down on the wall and thought about her predicament. Behind her, still stamping among the bushes, was Anna Beth's horse. Jo looked over her shoulder at it consideringly.

It was not tethered. It seemed as disturbed by the whole business as her own horse had been. Would it be possible to catch it and ride it back? 'Worth a try,' she said philosophically.

Very calmly and steadily she advanced upon the horse. Then she cursed. Anna Beth had chosen the rogue of the stables for her morning jaunt. Salome. That must have been why the stable-hands were so worried, Jo realised in a flash of enlightenment.

Salome looked back at her. She had intelligent, liquid eyes, and a way of lifting her top lip that made it look as if she was sneering. She also looked as if she had not had a good day so far, and was ready to take it out on the next stupid human who came her way.

'Believe me, sweetie, I don't blame you,' Jo assured her. She walked towards her, talking steadily in an even tone. 'Think of us as being in the same boat.'

The horse tossed her head.

The next few minutes were frustrating in the extreme. Whenever she got close enough to Salome to take her bridle, the horse twitched away and stood watching her, just out of reach. In the end, though, the horse seemed suddenly to get bored with the game. She let Jo get on her back with scarcely a protest.

'All right,' said Jo, taking the reins into her hands and patting Salome's neck experimentally. 'Where do you fancy? Up or down?'

The horse had no hesitation. She danced around on the spot, and then plunged back under the overhanging branches. Jo held on grimly, swinging to one side to avoid the lower ones, not sure if Salome was deliberately trying to scrape her off her back.

But they got back to the path and the horse turned confidently up towards the summit. Jo felt the surging power in the animal and took a policy decision to let her have her head.

Salome was not an easy ride, and Jo was breathless by the time they came within sight of the Land Rover. So she had no breath to answer when she was summoned with an imperious gesture.

'Where the hell have you been? Seb's been shouting down the phone. For Pete's sake let's get on with it,' said the old Englishman with the shoulder-balanced camera.

Salome danced sideways. She had the look of a horse who did not care for the internal combustion engine. Jo held on to her with hands that ached.

'But...'

The phone went again, with a buzz like an angry wasp.

The Land Rover's driver picked it up. 'Yes, she's here. What?' A pause. 'Fine, I think. Ready to go whenever you say. OK.'

He put the receiver down and turned to her. 'They've got the coach on the road. You just go over there, where they can see you, and start when you want. We keep behind you under the trees.'

Salome kicked irritably. The driver looked startled, but the cameraman was delighted. 'Looks ready for a gallop,' he said.

Jo gave in to the inevitable. She nodded, fighting the horse, and did her best to get the creature out on to the bluff the man had indicated.

Below her the little party around the first unit looked incredibly far away. The sun glinted on lenses and polished metal. It would be nice, thought Jo, hauling on Salome's reins for all she was worth, if she made it down to them in one piece.

She snatched a hand briefly off the reins, gave a wide, reckless wave, and let Salome go.

They thundered down the hill at a rate that Jo would not have thought was possible. Salome clearly knew her way. Jo kept her broadly in the middle of the open track, but it was not really necessary. As they skittered round a corner, a flurry of stones and dust shot up from her hooves.

There was a smooth curve of flat ground, almost a ride, round the spur of the hill. Salome was having none of it. She scrambled down the narrow, baked path, checking her pace only a little. Jo, recognising sure-footedness, began to relax. She still thought it would be a miracle if she got to the bottom, but at least the horse wasn't going to hurt herself.

But, amazingly, Salome took her down through the little group of olive trees, with Jo lying flat on her back and throwing herself sideways to avoid the branches they thundered under, and out on to the broad track where Bill and the coach were waiting.

If the mare hadn't had her gallop, Jo knew she would have had no chance of controlling her. But Salome had got rid of her surplus energy, along with a lot of her temper. She checked, in response to Jo's signal, and paced beside the coach.

Jo's breath was coming in deep gasps and her shoulders were aching. But one look at Bill's horrified face reminded her that the cameras were still running and she was supposed to be acting.

She looked doubtfully at the coach door. She was supposed to wrench it open. She was pretty sure that Salome had not calmed down enough to permit that. A tentative grab at it proved the truth of her conclusion.

Jo looked round wildly. What could she do now?

Bill was riding out ahead of the coach, shouting. Following his lead, Jo took Salome into the path of the coach, which slowed to a stop. Bill's face was white.

Salome, presumably detecting the end of her fun, decided to fling one last trick before she was imprisoned in her stable. She came up on her hind legs, and caracoled in front of the coach like a circus horse.

'Damn you, you vain, evil-minded, show-off,' Jo hissed, fighting grimly to stay on her back. 'This is not a cabaret. *Down*, for heaven's sake.'

The real fight had gone out of Salome, though. This last trick was pure high spirits. She came down on to all four legs, did a little sideways prance, just to prove who was in charge, and stood still. With a presence of mind which she was, afterwards, only able to marvel at, Jo pulled the pistol out of her belt as she had rehearsed and waved it vaguely in the direction of the coach.

'Cut!'

Never had a word been so welcome. Jo tumbled forwards on to the mare's neck, silky with sweat, gasping for breath. Salome stood virtuously still, as if she took four-year-olds on training rides every day of the week.

Running steps crunched on the uneven hillside. She was unceremoniously dragged from the horse's back. Her legs were shaking so much that she could only cling to the hard arms that were shaking her.

'And what the *bloody* hell was that all about?' Seb said bitingly.

His face, thought Jo, had lost all colour. It was interesting to see. She would not have thought a man so tanned and fit could look so ill. In the circumstances it was quite funny. She was the one who ought to look ill. She began to giggle weakly.

Crack! Jo stopped with a gasp. Seb had slapped her face. Not lightly.

'If you think hysterics is the answer, we're all entitled to join in,' he said savagely. 'If I can refrain from throwing my head back and howling like a banshee, you can damned well do the same.'

He shook her again. Jo felt her head wobble foolishly, and protested.

'Shut up,' Seb snapped; then, to someone else, 'Get that damned horse. Tie her up. Hobble her. Gag her. Do anything before she kills someone.'

Jo looked over her shoulder to where Salome looked mildly surprised to find herself in the middle of all the attention. Jo started to laugh but, with a wary eye on Seb, stopped abruptly.

Bill had swung off his horse and came over to them. From behind Seb's shoulder, he said anxiously, 'Are you all right?'

Jo nodded. She felt oddly disinclined to move out of the circle of Seb's punishing arms.

Bill drew a long breath. 'Thank goodness for that. When you came out of the trees like a bullet out of a gun, I thought you'd been bitten by a snake or some-thing. It was——'

'It was bloody irresponsible,' Seb said coldly. He held Jo away from him so that he could look down into her face. 'What *is* it with you?' he demanded, almost to himself. 'You know that that horse is valuable, I suppose? Do you know how much it would have cost if she'd been hurt?'

Jo's legs and her breathing were beginning to steady. A slow, burning anger began to rise. It was all too fam-iliar. She said sweetly, 'And if *I'd* been hurt?'

'Your own stupid fault, if you can't resist showing off for the cameras,' Seb said between his teeth.

Jo stepped smartly out of his arms. 'I see. So you stopped the cameras, did you? You saw how dangerous it was, and you said to them all, cut, we've got an emergency on our hands?' She was nearly spitting with rage.

Seb glared. 'I didn't tell you to get on a hot-blooded maniac and tear down the hill as if you were on skis. It was your own risk.'

'And no use to you.' Jo nodded with spurious sym-pathy. 'Poor old Seb. You'll have to do it all over again, with a nice easy cart-horse doing what you wanted. Everything I've done this morning of course is com-pletely wasted. It wasn't what you wanted, and it isn't any use.'

'I didn't say that.'

She took an impetuous step towards him and glared up into his furious face. 'No, you didn't. Because it isn't like that, is it, Seb? You can come and lecture me, high moral tone all round, but that didn't stop you *using* me.'

His eyes had narrowed to slits, and his mouth was a thin, vicious line. There was a splash of colour on the high cheekbones. 'If you ever say that to me again, I'll *use* you so you really know what it means,' he said barely above a whisper.

Bill looked alarmed. He touched him on the arm. 'Hang on there, Seb. You're both a bit wound up...'

'I am not,' said Seb Corbel freezingly, 'wound up. As the director of this movie, I am disgusted by Miss Page's self-indulgence and lack of professionalism.'

'Oh, is that what it is?' murmured Bill.

Neither Seb nor Jo took any notice of him.

'Well, if that's your idea of directing a colleague, I'm surprised that anyone will work with you, let alone put up the money for these extravaganzas,' Jo said viciously. 'I presume they don't do it twice?' She was shaking; with temper, she told herself. It had to be temper.

'You,' said Seb, very cold and quiet, 'are one hell-cat. It's time someone gave you the lesson you're asking for.'

Jo opened her mouth. But he was gone.

CHAPTER SEVEN

JO WAS still shaking when she got back to the wardrobe caravan. Lisa took one look at her and sat her down with a cup of freshly brewed coffee.

'He was worried,' she offered, as she began to ease the wig off.

'So was I,' snapped Jo. 'I was riding the creature.'

Lisa detached the wig and put it on its stand. 'Yes. I was wondering about that. It wasn't the old bay you started off with, was it?'

Jo gave a brief laugh. 'You noticed!' She shook out her own dark, short hair and ran angry fingers through it. 'How come he—nobody else did?'

'I used to be horse-mad,' Lisa said, 'when I was a child. And the one you rode is beautiful.'

'Her character, however, leaves much to be desired,' Jo said with feeling.

'Well, she's not alone in that,' Lisa said. 'Not in this film.'

Their eyes met in the mirror. Jo said hurriedly that she had to get back. Lisa gave a little nod, as if Jo had just confirmed something she had suspected.

At the house Jo went straight into a scented bath. She inspected herself carefully. She did not really expect bruises—the pain would come from her overstretched muscles. She sank her shoulders under the scented water and rotated them carefully. Her hands were sore too. Jo massaged them carefully, then did exercises she had learned at a riding school a couple of years ago.

It was then that she caught sight of the bruise on the inside of her wrist. Startled, she looked at the other one. It was the same, except that it showed the distinct impression of the cruel fingers.

Jo caught her breath. And he had the cheek to talk about teaching *her* a lesson.

She got out of the bath, dressed quickly and went downstairs. The staff were preparing the normal enormous lunch, but most of the film people were out on the hill. Carlos Andrade had come back, however.

Jo caught up with him exercising in the cool of a downstairs salon. He was making passes with a foil that glittered like a flake of diamond. She watched in silence for a bit before he caught sight of her and lowered the foil.

'That's going to be wonderful on film,' Jo said, strolling forwards.

Carlos looked pleased. He propped the foil carefully in the corner. 'I have wanted to see what could be done for years. In films, I mean. But until I met Seb I could never get anyone to take me seriously.'

Jo felt faintly alarmed. 'Are you telling me that you and I are going to have a serious fight?'

He grinned. 'I hope not.'

Jo gave an exaggerated sigh of relief. 'Well, thank goodness for that. I'm not up to your killer instinct.'

Carlos Andrade looked even more amused. 'I wouldn't have said that. Not after your death-defying ride this morning. The crew were impressed, Miguel tells me. Apparently, that horse eats stable-boys for breakfast. How did it feel?'

'Lively,' Jo said. She picked up the foil and tested its tip. 'If you're not having a proper fight with me, then who is?'

'Jackson Heald. You won't have heard of him. He used to be Canadian champion fifteen years ago. He's stunting for the guy who plays the uncle, and is arriving tomorrow.'

'They're certainly going for authenticity,' Jo said.

Andrade smiled. 'Seb,' he laid the slightest emphasis on the name, 'is like that. You should get on well together.'

Jo stiffened. 'Well, as you've seen, we don't,' she said curtly. 'Do you want to carry on, or do you feel like a drink?'

Andrade took the change of subject gracefully. 'Sangria,' he said. 'And afterwards, I thought I'd take one of the cars and tour round a bit. Do you know this area?'

They went out into the sunlight. Jo fished her sunglasses out of the pocket of her cotton skirt. She shook her head. 'Not at all. Do you?'

Andrade chuckled. 'When Brazilians come to Europe they go to Paris and London, maybe Madrid. Not the back of beyond, where the shopping's worse than at home.'

Jo laughed. 'Now you've reminded me; I ought to look out for something to take back for my grandfather.'

'Come with me,' Carlos Andrade offered casually. 'You can share the driving. I don't know which I hate most: the cars or the roads.'

So after lunch they borrowed a battered Fiat and set off through the gates of the hacienda, on to the metalled highway, Jo navigating.

The afternoon was completely still. They went through the village of Santa Ana at a crawl. Not so much as a cat stirred.

'Siesta,' said Andrade unnecessarily. 'Very civilised. Though the village is not big on mod cons. One of the boys was showing me where he's putting up. We've been lucky.'

'*I've* been lucky. I just picked up a room vacated by one of the stars. Up there,' Jo said, pointing. 'But you're a celebrity in your own right.'

Andrade said, 'You're too modest. *You're* a celebrity in your own field. Seb said . . .' But then he broke off, as if he had only just remembered that he did not want to repeat what Seb had said.

Jo could guess what it was. 'He's paying through the nose for me,' she said evenly. 'He resents it.'

Andrade did not deny it. 'I guess it got to him that you didn't want to work on his dream movie,' he said lightly.

Jo said, without thinking, 'If I hadn't needed the money, I wouldn't have. And I won't again.'

Andrade concentrated on the road. 'Ah,' he said.

Jo was shaken by the feeling in her voice. He must have heard it too. She said, 'I'm sorry. I didn't mean to spit. I don't normally take my temper out on by-standers. It's just that Seb Corbel has been shouting at me ever since I arrived. And I'm tired of it.'

'Yes,' he said. 'I noticed that he got pretty steamed up over you.' He looked at her sideways. 'Seb doesn't normally blow his cool. Not his image at all.'

'Nor do I,' said Jo with dignity.

There was a pause. Then, 'You seem to have a lot in common,' murmured Andrade.

'Mutual loathing,' Jo returned.

'Ah,' he said again. And changed the subject.

They went to a little beach-side town, and swam. Then they had coffee, and swam again, before drifting round the little booths as they opened after the siesta. Andrade bought a mantilla for his girlfriend. Jo found an old map that she thought her grandfather would like.

Jo drove back. Santa Ana had woken up by the time they got there; the two bars were open, with men sitting on the wooden chairs under the awnings. Somebody was plucking at a guitar.

Andrade cocked his head as they drove carefully through the tiny street. 'Practising, do you think?'

Jo listened. 'It sounds pretty professional to me.'

'Yes, but there's a competition tonight. One of the big ones.'

'Really?' She was interested. 'Surely not here, in Santa Ana. It's so tiny.'

'More romantic than that. Up in the hills. Some sort of gypsy meeting. It happens every year.' He looked straight ahead up the twisting road, and said coolly, 'You should get Seb to tell you about it.'

'Seb?'

'He's an expert. He always comes to these gypsy fiestas. That's how he found this place to begin with. And it's why the publishers let him have the rights to the film. Because he really cared. Because he would do it properly.'

'I didn't know.'

'There's a lot you don't know about Seb,' Andrade said drily. 'You ought to find out.'

Jo did not know how to answer. So she said nothing. After a quick sideways look, he did not pursue it either.

She left him with thanks, and went straight to her room.

She sank down in the chair in front of the dressing-table and looked at herself. Was Andrade right? Were she and Seb Corbel alike? And was she really so ignorant of him? If so, why did it feel as if she had known him all her life? And why did he affect her so strongly?

The answer was all too obvious. Sexual attraction, Jo told herself unhappily, staring at her pale face in the mirror. That's what it was. Dammed up for years, and how unleashed; now, when she was tired, and worried, and nearly at the end of her tether. When she got home it would wear off.

Temporary and unpleasant, she told herself, remembering how her blood thundered at his smallest touch; how she almost always knew when he was there. She wondered whether he reacted to her unseen presence in the same way, and then took herself to task: this was the stuff of fantasy. Indulging it was not sensible, and it wouldn't help her to get over this silly physical attraction when she eventually went back to normality.

It was crazy. Something was happening to her. Maybe she had just come to some sort of crisis in her life. After all, look at how she had reacted to her glimpse of Anna Beth's embrace with the gypsy. I'm turning into a frustrated spinster, Jo thought, getting fixated on whatever man is available. The sooner I get away the better. It left her feeling desolate.

It was just as well that Miguel put his head round her french window.

'Feeling better?' he asked cheerfully.

'You mean, have I recovered from that nightmare of a ride?' Jo asked wryly. 'Or Seb's professional reprimand?'

Miguel made a sympathetic noise. 'Forget it. Let me kidnap you for the evening.'

With an effort, Jo smiled. 'Sounds exciting.'

He gave her a droll look. 'I hope so. It's the local flamenco festival. We listen to the music out on the hill. There's a barbecue of sorts. We take what we want to drink, and dance, if we feel like it. Do you know how to do the *sevillanas*?'

Jo shook her head.

'Well, after enough Rioja, you'll learn fast enough. Just don't wear trousers. And bring a shawl. The party goes on all night; it can get cold.'

Jo hesitated. 'Will Anna Beth be there?'

Miguel made a face. 'Dancing with gypsies in the open air?'

But it was a gypsy that she had lured, laughing, along the veranda that night.

Seeing her hesitation, Miguel said, 'Come on, Jo. It won't do any good to sit and sulk.'

So she shrugged, and went. She had to borrow a full, tiered cotton skirt from one of the maids. It swirled out horizontally, as high as her waist if she pirouetted fast enough, as the girl demonstrated cheerfully. Jo resolved to be careful.

But Miguel was right. It was a relief not to be eating in that populous courtyard, not when they had all heard the dressing-down Seb had given her, never even asking for her side of the story. How that must have delighted Anna Beth.

She was there this evening. She too was obviously going out somewhere later. She was wearing slim, sophisticated black, tight-fitting, with a subtly curved and cut bodice, so that it looked modest while contriving access to a considerable amount of creamy flesh. And her diamonds were magnificent.

She gave Jo a smile that just teetered on the edge of smugness. 'Going out with the boys, honey?' The pansy eyes considered and dismissed the pretty embroidered shirt that was Jo's own, and the borrowed fall of jade and peacock cotton. 'Enjoy yourself.'

Anna Beth was waving them away as Seb appeared from the house. He was himself again, laid back and laughing. He did not even check when he saw Jo with

Miguel and Carlos Andrade, who had decided to join them. Seb was still in his working jeans and dusty shirt.

'Not eating?' he said, tucking a clipboard under his arm and smiling at them.

'Darling, they're going native. They'll get some popcorn at the game, or whatever it is,' Anna Beth said. Her pretty tone did not quite disguise the spite.

Miguel said equably, 'That's about the size of it. The fiesta. Coming, Seb?'

Anna Beth frowned quickly. 'We're going to see some people.'

Seb's eyes narrowed. He did not answer, but he and Miguel exchanged a look which made Jo stiffen. Anna Beth, however, appeared not to notice. She stretched like a pedigree cat and put a hand, with delicately painted nails, on Seb's arm. 'Darling?'

Seb said to Miguel in an even tone, 'Don't keep the girl dancing all night. I've got work for her.'

'In bed by midnight,' Miguel asured him blithely and swept Jo, in her borrowed skirts, out of the lights of the courtyard and into the night. She knew that Seb watched them go.

The journey into the mountains, with Miguel driving, was hair-raising. Jo tried to concentrate on his lecture on flamenco, and to forget the occasional glimpse of the lake, further and further below them, as he swung blithely round the next hairpin bend.

But he got them there.

It was a piece of flat ground where there were a number of vehicles pulled up already. It was full of a sense of expectancy. All around them people were plucking at guitars, tuning them, shaking out new strings. Women were pulling their full-skirted dresses straight and patting their hair into place. In the distance Jo could see a substantial bonfire.

'Barbecue,' Miguel said, jerking his head in the direction of the smoke. 'Later. But there will be tapas now.'

And, indeed, there were—boys of ten or eleven were circulating with woven baskets and trays full of the delicious snacks. Jo ate garlicky toast, delicious little slivers of sardine on bread, olives and smoky sausage. Carlos and Miguel appeared to be making a hearty meal.

They installed themselves under a tree, opened a bottle of wine, and waited.

For about half an hour the scene was unchanged as people continued to arrive. Clearly most of them knew other people in the gathering. Clearly, also, nobody knew Miguel. It made no difference. They were greeted with grave courtesy, and one or two of the guitar players and dancers had a glass of wine with them under their tree.

For the first time for days, it seemed to Jo, she relaxed in the smoky darkness. Soon people began to draw into a circle, and the strumming became less tentative and jumbled. Eventually a man ran into the centre of the circle and began to sing. Even though Jo did not understand the words, it was strangely haunting to watch.

It was soon apparent that there were three sorts of songs: sad, almost oriental laments; lively explosions of pleasure; and the brooding tales of passion, love and revenge. Miguel translated some of them but he did not really need to.

One or two of the tunes were familiar, but most were strange, odd half-lines of melody mingled with Arab harmonies and percussive hand rhythms. It was wild and fierce and exhilarating.

'We could be on another planet,' Jo said wonderingly. 'I've never heard anything like it. It's so formal—*proud*—and yet so absolutely emotional.'

'Basic, Seb calls it,' Miguel said.

She could no longer make out more than the shape of his shoulders and profile in the scented dark. But she could hear the grin in his voice.

'He's right,' she said, animosity forgotten. 'It's so—moving. I'll never forget this, Miguel. Thank you for bringing me.'

'Wait until the dancing starts before you thank me,' he advised.

But there was more singing first; more intricate and passionate guitar music; more of the display-dancing by the strong, dignified people who had talked to them in the firelight.

The flaming torches began to gutter and were replaced. As they died in a swirl of pine-scented smoke, the scene seemed to dance before Jo's eyes.

She leaned against Miguel's shoulder and said, 'I've drunk too much wine. I ought to go back.'

But Miguel only said, 'You can't have done. And you haven't danced yet. You can't go. It's rude.'

So she didn't. And then the dancing began.

Almost at once an elderly man danced with her. He thanked her gravely and handed her on to a group of girls, who soon had her whirling among them in a pattern-dance. Jo began to feel positively light-headed from the music, the wine and the strange wavering light.

And then it happened. Out of the shadows, and the foggy haze that was the bonfire, stepped the gypsy. She knew him at once. She knew the set of the shoulders, the whole shape of his body. She stared at him, transfixed.

He came across the clearing to her with long, graceful strides. Jo was rooted to the spot. That air of animal vitality just held in check was terrifying. Yet she could not tear her eyes away from the dark figure. She put a hand to her throat where her pulse was fluttering madly.

Why was he coming to her? Had he seen her watching him and Anna Beth that night? Seen her turn tail and flee from their uninhibited pleasure in each other?

The breath caught in Jo's throat at the thought. She turned in a whisk of frills and dived among the crowd.

Even though she did not look back, she could feel him following, feel him bearing down on her like something out of a dream. Her mouth dried. She looked around for the others but she saw, in the wavering light, that Miguel was dancing and Carlos Andrade was deep in conversation.

She retreated deeper into the dark. A hand closed on her shoulder. Jo froze.

Behind them, the music went through one of its abrupt changes of tone and tempo. The clapping became faster and more insistent. The shadows swirled wildly as the dancers stamped faster and faster round the bonfire.

'Dance.' It was a breath, no more, in her ear. It was also a command, not an invitation.

Not looking round, Jo said rapidly in a low voice, 'I'm very sorry, I don't know how...'

But the long fingers had already turned her forcefully and the gypsy was guiding her body to follow his own, with its swaying step, into the dancing crowd. Jo felt the strength. Crazily, it almost felt familiar. She kept her eyes on the pale glimmer of his shirt. But she did not resist.

The strange, alien music tugged at her. She found herself moving easily with him to its rhythm. He said something under his breath. She looked up, but his face was a shadow among shadows. All around them other dancers were moving with their proud, stamping steps to the driving music. The clever fingers spun her away from him and, almost before she was aware, pulled her back, curving her arm high over her head, their hands locked. It was perfect physical co-ordination. At the implication of that harmony, Jo caught her breath again. Above her, the gypsy laughed softly.

And then the music changed again. The stamping and clapping stopped, and the sound dwindled to a single guitar, playing in the minor key, piercingly sad. The dancers began to move slowly, dreamily; the women almost stationary, the men stalking proudly around them. Jo's heart began to hammer.

As swiftly as he had taken her among the dancers, he swept her out of the crowd into the darkness under the olive trees. Jo went as if she were in a dream.

The earth was uneven beneath their feet. Twigs cracked under their steps. Once, his hand tightened as she half turned her foot. He righted her, swiftly, pulling her back against his body to do so. Jo felt his heart thundering under her shoulder-blade. She gave an unmistakable shiver. His heartbeat quickened. He urged her on faster.

At last they were in a clearing. The music was a distant echo. The guitar was plaintive and clear, but the voices, the percussion and the frenzied sense of excitement were no more than a memory. Except, thought Jo, as she turned into his arms, that this was an altogether deeper and more disturbing excitement.

Afterwards, she could not remember whether he had drawn her round to face him or if she had turned of her own accord. She knew that her breath was quick and shallow, and that she had never been more frightened in her life. At the same time, there was nothing she could do. She felt as if that lowering figure, darker than the surrounding darkness under the still trees, had been waiting for her all her life. With the inevitability of a dream, she reached up for his kiss.

He said something in Spanish with a rough husky voice. That, too, seemed familiar. And then he was kissing her with a hunger he did not even try to disguise.

Jo's head fell back. His mouth moved over her cheek, her closed eyelids. The long fingers were at the nape of her neck, infinitely tender. Her heart began to slam against her ribs.

'This is crazy,' she said. It was no more than a breath.

He murmured against her skin. She could not make out the words.

Struggling for sanity, she said, 'I don't want...'

But his hand swept the length of her spine, drawing her hard against him in one fluid movement. Jo gasped as if she had been burned.

In the distance the guitars mourned in the minor key, wailing above the steady, stamping percussion.

Held against that warm strength, she was on an uncharted sea. The drumming beat drove through her body, wave after drowning wave. Oh, lord, she thought. This happened to other people. Not to scared Jo Page, in her armour.

'I've never...' she said desperately, half to herself.

But he did not seem to hear. He kissed her mouth, and something inside her flamed up to answer that terrifying domination. She kissed him back, almost angrily.

For a wild instant they clung to each other. Jo thought she would remember it forever: the smell of the wood smoke and the olives; the insistent rhythm of the distant guitars and their own driving pulses; the friendly darkness. She was shaking with panic and her own, unexpected passion.

He said something, half whispering, half laughing, against her skin. She was so bewildered, she did not even know what language he used.

Then, in the trees, not very far from them, she heard voices she knew. She froze in the gypsy's arms.

'I shall do what I like,' Anna Beth Arden was saying defiantly.

The gypsy seemed unaware of them. He ran his hands over and over Jo's hip-bones, as if he were stroking a cat.

Someone—was it Simon?—was saying, 'It's going to be tough, tomorrow.'

'Not,' said Anna Beth, sounding spiteful, 'for me.'

Jo tried in vain to draw away. She was tremulous with pleasure under the deliberate caress. She heard the answer remotely. It did not seem to have much to do with her, in this turmoil of feeling, or the man in whose arms she stood.

The others were coming closer. The gypsy ran his lips lightly along the line of Jo's eyebrow. She felt his breath, warm and faintly smoky, against her face. The sensation was so sweet that she smothered a gasp.

At once the approaching footsteps halted.

'What's that?' Simon said sharply.

'Lovers, I bet.' Anna Beth did not sound kind. 'Shall we go see?'

Simon protested; but his horror was nothing compared with Jo's. It brought her down to earth with a bump. Suddenly the magic dissolved and she saw herself standing in the dark, on a foreign hillside, clasped in the arms of a man she would not even recognise if she saw him by day. She gave one horrified gasp and wrenched herself free.

The gypsy was unprepared, and his caressing hands did not catch her back to him quickly enough. With a little sob of dismay, Jo flung herself blindly away and ran in the direction of the music.

CHAPTER EIGHT

THE bonfire was easy to find. Jo could smell the smoke even before she saw the flickering flames in the distance. She stumbled towards it, panting.

What had happened to her? She put both hands to her trembling mouth. It did not feel like her own. And her heart was pounding in her breast like a terrified animal's.

She stopped on the edge of the clearing, her hand to her side. She could not see either Carlos or Miguel. In fact, she could not see anything very clearly. Impatient with herself, she shook her head. Was sensible, well-defended Jo Page going to fall apart because a man she did not know kissed her in the darkness, under the trees?

Ah, but she felt as if she did know him. As if she had known him for a hundred years. As if her body had been waiting for just those hands, just this night. She moistened dry lips.

And, in that moment, heard herself hailed.

'Jo! Over here! *Jo!*'

It was Carlos Andrade. Jo turned towards him. She still felt dazed.

He came up to her, looking at her curiously. 'Are you all right?'

She became aware that her hand was still pressed to her side. Hurriedly she took it away. 'Of course.'

She could hardly make out his slim figure in the smoke-filled darkness. But she could sense his concern.

'Sure?'

Jo gave a swift nod. 'Just a bit of a stitch,' she improvised. Even to her own ears it sounded thin. Her voice wobbled on the brave words.

But Carlos was convinced, and laughed. 'That's what comes of trying to keep up with the experts. Seb must be in the same condition.' He took her arm. 'Come on, lean on me. I'll find you a nice safe log to sit on and a drink.'

'No,' said Jo instinctively.

Carlos stopped, looking down at her in surprise. Even knowing that he could not see her expression, Jo covered her hot cheeks with her hands.

'I mean—I'm tired. That's all. I want to go home.'

Home, she thought. That was exactly where she wanted to go. Away from this film with its temperaments and its uncertainties. Away from the gypsy and whatever it was that he called to in herself. Above all, away from Seb. Before she had known Seb and his lazy, penetrating perception, would she have fallen, drowning, into the gypsy's embrace?

Carlos said slowly, 'I thought you were enjoying yourself.'

'I was. I did.' Why, oh, why did she have to sound like a desperate schoolgirl? 'Only I've got to work tomorrow and——'

'And the dancing has worn you out.' She could almost hear the shrug in his voice. He looked round. 'Well, Seb must be going back soon. You can hitch a ride with him.'

Seb?

'*No,*' she said on an indrawn breath of pure horror.

She thought of his lazy, perceptive eyes and her crazy awareness of him. She was in no state to meet him now, raw and bewildered from her encounter with the gypsy.

She looked at the little cluster of lights to be seen, beyond the bonfire, halfway down the mountain: Santa Ana.

'I can walk,' she said. 'There's a track. And I won't get lost. I can see the village all the way.'

'You'll break your neck.' Carlos, a townsman, sounded genuinely horrified.

Shaken though she was, Jo laughed. By the fire someone had started to sing again, accompanied by fierce hand-clapping and those driving guitars.

'Not me,' she said with confidence.

'Even so—what would Seb say...?'

That caught her on the raw. 'Seb is not my keeper,' she flashed.

'Have you told him that?' Carlos sounded mildly amused. 'Is that why you were standing there looking pole-axed?'

Bewildered, Jo stared at him. He patted her hand.

'It's all right. I won't tell. It's your business.'

She said slowly, 'What are you talking about, Carlos?'

He shrugged. 'Just that I saw you. Together,' he explained with heavy sarcasm. 'Tonight. And Seb didn't look as if he was going to let you walk home on your own,' he added drily.

Jo shook her head. 'I——'

'As I said. Your business. No need to make up lies for my benefit. Don't have to tell me anything.'

'I don't lie,' she flashed. 'Whoever you saw, it wasn't me. I've——' She bit it off. 'Well, I was with some other people,' she ended lamely. 'You were mistaken. Maybe it was Anna Beth. I heard her voice a while ago. She must have changed her mind.'

'Maybe.' He sounded as if he didn't believe her but couldn't be bothered to argue. Jo also had the distinct impression that he was amused at something—what, she could not guess.

The wailing voice ended. The dancers were swirling up again, brushing Jo's shoulder as they passed. In the confusion, Carlos dropped her arm. Jo stepped back and saw him claimed by a shadowy girl with a dress that the firelight revealed as ruby-red. He went, good-humouredly, though he looked over his shoulder as if he wanted to keep her in his sights. Jo melted into the shadows.

As she had expected, the walk was easy. It was not even very far. From Santa Ana to the hacienda the road was metalled. In the starlight it was as clear as a ribbon of black velvet. From above, the faint rhythms seemed to billow out of the hillside with the smoke, Jo thought.

The house was quiet and all but in darkness. A single light still burned on the little staircase by Anna Beth's room. Jo went up it and along the gallery on silent feet. There were no lights in any of the rooms she passed. Either everyone was at the fiesta or asleep.

She slipped out of her clothes and fell into bed without turning on her own light. She was, she told herself, exhausted.

She was still saying it when, hours later, she heard the others arrive back. There was a muted hum of voices, steps trying to be quiet, a light snapped on and as quickly off when someone protested. They all sounded very happy, she thought, turning for the twentieth time and thumping her pillow.

There was a soft tread along the gallery. It stopped outside her french windows. As always she had left them ajar. Her skin prickled with familiar awareness. She did not need to ask who was standing there. She held her breath.

'Jo.' It was hardly more than a sigh.

She lay rigid and did not answer. If he thought she was asleep he would go away. Surely he would go away.

He pushed open the doors and edged his way noiselessly into the room. Her hands curled into tight fists; her short nails dug into the soft flesh of her palm like talons. With all her might Jo willed him to go away. She could not bear this. She *could* not. She screwed her eyes tight shut.

For a tense and frightful minute she lay there, knowing that he was looking at her. Then, with a small sigh, he turned and went.

The tension went out of her in a great wave. And it was then that Jo began to cry.

She fell asleep, of course. Eventually. Her eyes gritty with crying, she just subsided into unconsciousness like an exhausted swimmer.

The nightmare came back slowly. It had never been like this before. Even asleep, Jo knew it. Even as she felt her limbs turn to iron and lose the ability to run, she knew that she had been here before and that this was worse than it had ever been.

In the distance a guitar was thrumming with the beat of a human heart. The man was there, watching her, closing in on her. Her lungs refused to work, as they always did. But this time the guitar grew louder, faster, drowning the little sounds she managed to force out of her parched throat. The man's breathing was loud in the silent room. But he was closer than he had ever been; suffocatingly close. As Jo struggled to wake up, she heard the angry blood pulsing through the reaching, greedy hands.

With a wrenching effort she flung herself sideways. It was no use. She did not move. Whimpering, she lay waiting for the end.

There was another noise, a voice, low but insistent.

'Wake up, Jo. It's a dream. Wake up. You're all right.'

She was desperate. She could not move a hand to defend herself.

'Wake *up*!'

Suddenly she was being shaken. Her shoulders were cold. Hands held her: not the creeping hands of her dream but a powerful grip that seemed to be dragging her bodily out of the nightmare.

Jo forced open her heavy eyelids. The shadow lowered over her, her nightmare turned into reality, and she fell back with a harsh indrawn breath that was shocking in the dark silence. She turned her head away, crouching back among the pillows.

The shadow straightened slowly. As she came fully awake she realised, too late, that she had betrayed herself. He must have heard her cry out. She hadn't cried out for years, but tonight's was bad. And Seb must have heard and come into her room to help—and she had reacted as if he were the horror itself.

She fell back among the maltreated pillows, her breath coming in painful gasps as she fought for composure.

'Well,' Seb said at last, slowly, 'at least you're alive. I thought you were dying back there for a while.'

Jo swallowed. 'Was I screaming?' she asked in a small voice.

'Rather the reverse. When I first heard it, I thought someone was trying to smother you. That's why I came in. Then I wondered about asthma?' he ended on a note of query.

Jo shook her head.

Seb sat down on the edge of the bed. He was barefoot and bare-chested and his hair was tousled, she saw. She must have woken him up. She imagined him leaping naked out of bed and hurrying into the black trousers before coming to her, and her cheeks flamed.

Seb leaned forwards and she tensed. But he made no attempt to touch her; he was just putting on the bedside light. He scanned her flushed face, taking in the hurried breathing and the wide, distressed eyes. There was a little silence.

'So—what was it? Too much Rioja and bonfire smoke?' he asked, almost idly.

Jo's throat was painful. She shook her head again, reaching for the bottle of mineral water that stood on the bedside table. Seb reached it before she did and opened it with a flick of the wrist that was almost violent. The sudden hiss was loud in the silence. Jo jumped. He registered that too and his lips tightened.

He poured her a glass and held it to her lips. She cupped her hands round the glass. They were shaking so she was grateful for his steadying fingers, though she took care not to touch them.

'A dream?'

She sat up and let her head fall back against the bedhead. 'Yes.'

'Bad.' It wasn't a question.

Jo's smile was a travesty and she knew it. 'Exceptional.'

'Ah.' Seb looked down at her for a moment. Then he leaned forwards and put the glass down on the table with exaggerated care. 'Recurring?'

'Yes.'

Another, longer silence. In the room, the whole house, there was not a murmur, not a movement. It was as if they were the last two people left alive on a devastated planet.

He said, 'Do you talk about it?'

She could not speak. She shook her head, eyes still holding the remembered horror.

He shifted his weight, clasping his hands round one knee. He looked, Jo thought, as if he was ready to sit there till morning.

'Inheritance from childhood?' Seb asked, still in that idle voice. But his eyes were watchful.

Jo made her rusty voice work. 'In a way.'

'Do you know the root of it?'

The curtains at the open window were stirring faintly in the breeze. It must be nearly dawn, Jo thought, watching them. Not taking her eyes off the filmy material she said, 'Oh, yes.'

'Then isn't it time you told?' Seb said drily. 'Or do you *want* people rushing into your bedroom with respirators?'

She shuddered. He drew a quick breath.

But all he said was, 'What happens? You're running away?'

Suddenly it didn't seem important to lock it away any more. Jo felt oddly as if the worst had happened and there was nothing more she could do.

She said, 'No. I can't move.'

Seb nodded; polite interest, nothing more. She looked away.

'I'm in bed,' she said remotely. 'Nearly asleep. I hear someone—him—breathing.'

He moved and was quickly still. 'I came in earlier. You—I thought you were asleep.'

'I know.'

'I—see.' He paused. Jo studied the still curtains as if her life depended on it. He probed gently, 'Is that it? You hear him breathing? That's all?'

'No.' Jo swallowed, her breathing hurried. 'Look, you can't be interested and I'm awake now and——'

His face was unreadable. He ignored her protest. 'So he's breathing. Then what?'

She was breathing in painful gasps now. She shook her head.

The inexorable voice, still without emotion, went on. 'He stabs you? Smothers you? Strangles you?'

'No,' she got out, a hand at her throat.

Seb reached out and took the hand in his own. He held it, looking at her gravely. 'Tell me, Jo. Then forget it. What does he do?'

'He—touches—me,' she whispered. 'He lies down and—crawls over me...' Her mouth began to shake. She pressed her free hand to her lips. 'Whispering all the time; that I mustn't make a noise; that I like it.'

The hand holding hers was suddenly a vice. But all he said was, 'Nasty.'

She felt his eyes on her. At last he said, with a quietness that was almost reluctant, 'Who?' And when she shook her head, 'You know, don't you? You have to know.'

She shut her eyes. Her teeth were clenched so hard that her jaw hurt.

'It started when you were a child,' that inexorable voice went on. 'How much of a child, Jo?'

'Thirteen.' It was a ragged whisper.

He nodded, seemingly unaware of the effort it cost her. 'So who were you living with when you were thirteen, Jo?'

The silence lengthened endlessly. He said nothing more, nor did he move. He just sat holding her hand as if he would stay there till doomsday.

Very slowly Jo opened her eyes and met his. In the half-light he looked very severe. Unconsciously she was hanging on to his hand like a lifeline.

'My mother's husband,' she said at last.

Seb said nothing. He sat like a rock.

Jo steadied her voice somehow. 'He was younger than she was. They used to fight. If John really wanted to hurt, he used to say he was young enough to be her son. Then—he started saying he'd divorce her and marry me.

'One day they had a really terrible scene. I was home from school. She sent me to my room. I was supposed to rest after the journey but really it was so they could carry on shouting at each other. I fell asleep and... and——'

'And when you woke up he was proving his point,' Seb said drily.

Jo winced. 'You could put it like that.'

The hand holding hers tightened. He said very gently, 'So what happened then? Did you call out? Another big scene?'

'No. I sort of wriggled away. And I was crying. I think he—well, he was drunk before but I think that shocked him a bit. He let me go in the end. Made me promise I wouldn't tell.'

'Did he try it again?' Seb asked evenly.

She swallowed. 'No. But I was never——'

'Never sure he wouldn't. No, I can see that.' He sounded almost absent. 'So you let it haunt you instead.'

Jo said bitterly, 'It didn't exactly ask my permission.'

Seb gave her a level look. 'You could have told. Oh, not then, maybe. But later. What about boyfriends? Lovers? Surely they had a right to know?'

Jo said nothing. For a moment he stared at her.

Then he said softly, 'Oh, no.'

She seized the water glass again and drank, concentrating. She could feel the intensity of his eyes on her. She would not look up.

'No boyfriends,' Seb said resignedly. 'So presumably nothing more grown up, either. What the hell did you do, Jo Page? Punish yourself for what happened? Put yourself in prison for life?'

She did not look at him then. Her breathing was back to normal and she felt an odd calm. 'No,' she said quietly. 'Not prison. Sanctuary.'

When he left her, Jo gave up the attempt to sleep. He had been kind, she thought ruefully, but there had been a distinct constraint in him. Presumably he was annoyed that the perfect robot turned out to have as much temperament as his highly prized actors. That had to be the reason for the anger she sensed in him.

She got up and dressed in her tracksuit and went out on to the terrace. Last night's lamp was still burning. In the sky the first fingers of sunlight were beginning to point up from the horizon. She put on her trainers and let herself out of the house.

Jo set off at her usual steady pace. To her dismay, the calm that usually descended on her when she began to run evaded her. What was happening to her?

It had all started when she came to Spain. She had been all right until then. Even putting together the money to buy Grandpa's house back for him hadn't worried her. She had been working hard, maybe too hard. But she had not felt this awful panicky sense of being about to shatter into little pieces.

Ever since Simon had met her at the airport—her thoughts broke off and she almost stumbled. No, not since Simon had met her; since Seb Corbel had come steaming up the steps to the little roof terrace in Santa Ana. That was when it had started: the breathless feeling of being on a precipice; of being under threat; of not knowing what anyone was going to say or do next—not even herself; of being more alive than she had ever been before in her life. And more afraid.

Jo slowed to a walk. Seb Corbel. He didn't like her. He had challenged her from the moment they had met. And she did not like him or the type of man he was.

So why did she feel that she knew him as well as he knew herself? Yet at the same time he was an absolute stranger, as unpredictable as the gods. And why did she always know when he was there? What strange magnetism was it that meant that he could not come into a room without her being aware of him?

She dropped on to a rock and sat, shivering a little, her arms clasped round herself.

The girls at school had talked about falling in love—with their brothers' friends, with their ski instructors. When she had had it described to her, Jo had said contemptuously that it sounded a complete pantomime. The girls—and their brothers' friends and ski instructors too—had been impressed by her loftiness, she remembered wryly.

Well, she was well served now. She knew nothing about love: was this it? This crazy desire to run when he was there—and hopeless incompleteness when he was not?

It was not a happy thought. He was not for her. She had the sense to realise that, Jo told herself. Even if the whole business of love and marriage had not terrified her, she would not have anything to offer the brilliant and ambitious Seb Corbel.

She sat bolt upright, suddenly noticing: the *whole* business? Love and *marriage*?

'I must be out of my mind,' Jo said, jumping up.

And she ran the rest of the way as if she were in a race with the devil.

That, of course, meant that she was not on top form when filming started. She tried to disguise her tiredness. In general she thought she succeeded. Lisa certainly noticed nothing. Nor did Simon.

Seb, of course, was different. He had not yet demanded a full explanation of her appearance on Salome, and Jo braced herself. But as always he did the unexpected.

'I told you so,' he said, looking her over casually.

Jo began to bristle. 'Told me what?'

'Exhaustion,' he drawled. 'You look half dead. Don't take any risks today, hmm? Remember my insurance— and my blood-pressure.'

Jo sighed. 'I've told you . . .'

He lifted one long-fingered hand lazily. 'I know. I know. You wear a parachute to bed in case you fall out.' He paused. 'Maybe you do, at that.'

Jo glared at him. Seb met her eyes squarely, his mouth wry. Without her quite knowing why, her own eyes fell. She could feel her colour rising. It did nothing to soothe her temper.

For some reason she thought sharply of the gypsy's hands on her last night. Her blush intensified. She bit her lip.

Seb watched her curiously. She gritted her teeth and reached for some sort of professional composure. 'I know what I'm doing,' she said at last.

Seb gave a dry laugh. He shook his head slowly. 'I very much doubt it,' he said in a voice that only she could hear.

Jo looked round. Anna Beth was reclining on a window-seat. She was talking to Simon but her eyes were fixed on Seb and Jo.

Jo decided not to take issue with his last remark. She pretended not to have heard.

Seb sighed, but all he said was, 'Carlos will take you through the moves of the fight. I've left it to him. He knows what I want.' He nodded at the staircase down which they were to have their famous encounter. 'Couple of silhouettes through the door at the end of the gallery. And a stand-off at the top of the flight before the last bout. He disarms you on the fourth step. OK?'

'I'll run through it with him,' she agreed. 'Sounds straightforward.'

'Give it your best.' He looked at his watch. 'We'll want you in, say, an hour.'

He caught Simon's eye and they went off. Anna Beth continued to watch Jo, her brown eyes narrowed. Then she stood up and strolled over.

Jo watched her warily. Normally Anna Beth went wherever Seb did. And he would be filming Bill swinging down the curtains in the drawing-room for the next hour.

Anna Beth stood in front of her and looked her up and down. 'Breeches don't really suit you,' she said at last, wrinkling her nose. 'They make you look like a boy.'

Jo raised her brows. 'Isn't that the point?'

Anna Beth laughed complacently. 'It confuses the audience. Now me—they know I'm a girl no matter what I'm wearing.'

In spite of her tiredness, Jo found she was amused. 'They would,' she agreed gravely.

Anna Beth knew she was being laughed at and she didn't like it. 'You think you're so damned clever,' she said on a hissing note. 'Don't you forget, this is *my* picture. I'm the star. You're nothing without me.'

For once there was a note of barely repressed hysteria in her voice. Jo was concerned. The beautiful face was pinched and there was a hint of wildness in Anna Beth's spiteful expression.

'Of course,' Jo began in a soothing voice but was overridden.

'You've been plotting ever since you arrived. Don't think I haven't seen it. The way you make up to him. The way you stole my scene, my ride...' Her voice rose.

Jo took a brisk step forwards and took hold of her wrists. 'Stop it,' she said sharply. 'I stole nothing. You're working yourself up for nothing.'

'You did. You did. You've hated me...'

Jo gave her a little shake. 'The boot's on the other foot,' she said. And as Anna Beth continued to rail at her she said in a calm, carrying voice, 'Listen to me. You know as well as I do what happened over that damned ride. The whole crew knows it was you who took Salome out. The stable-boys told them. I don't know what they think about how we managed to change horses, but I bet they've got a shrewd idea.'

Anna Beth fell silent, her eyes full of tears. But the look she gave Jo was calculating.

'No, I haven't told anyone,' Jo said. 'But if you don't stop this silly behaviour I will. I'll tell them all. Seb,' she said with great deliberation, 'first.'

Anna Beth's face was venomous. Jo was momentarily startled by the sheer fury in it. But then the girl broke away from her.

'It's only your word against mine.'

Jo allowed herself a small smile. 'Exactly. Who do you think they'll believe?'

'But it's *my picture*,' Anna Beth said, bewildered.

Jo laughed aloud.

'It is. My husband——'

'Your husband may have put up some of the money. But the film won't happen without actors, technicians, musicians. Above all, the director. If it's anybody's film, it's Seb Corbel's,' Jo said with brutal frankness.

Anna Beth drew a little hissing breath. 'You've been chasing him ever since you got here,' she flung at Jo. 'Getting him in corners. Telling him lies about me.'

Jo turned away in disgust.

'Don't turn your back on me!' Anna Beth shouted. 'I know what you're up to...'

Jo shrugged. 'You're crazy,' she said without looking round.

She did not wait to hear Anna Beth's answer to that. She ran lightly up the curving staircase and went in search of Carlos Andrade.

He was in the billiard-room, practising precision lunges. He too was in costume, although he was not yet wearing the heavy coat and plumed hat that she knew were waiting for him.

'Very handsome,' Jo said, strolling in a little out of breath.

He turned and grinned, shaking out his ruffles. 'I could get used to it. They must have been a bunch of peacocks.' He stood his foil carefully in the corner and came over to her.

'Seb said you'd take me through the fight.'

Carlos nodded. 'I've roughed out a few suggestions.' He gestured at a piece of paper on the fireplace. 'Do you want to try it out?'

'At half speed,' said Jo, casting a quick eye over it, 'it looks perfectly manageable.'

He picked up his foil again and tossed her its fellow. They went through the moves he had written. Carlos was formidably strong but he was a clear, competent teacher and did not push her. After a while he announced himself to be pleased.

'You're good,' he said, passing her a glass of orange juice.

Jo shook her head, laughing. 'Not enough practice.'

'No. But you're fast and you've got a good eye. That's important. And you keep your cool.'

'That,' said Jo, trickling orange juice gratefully down her throat, 'is part of the trade. Though I'm afraid I wasn't very cool this morning,' she added thoughtfully.

He looked enquiring. She told him about her encounter with Anna Beth. He looked disgusted. 'That girl is paranoid. Goodness knows why Seb puts up with it.'

Jo raised her eyebrows. He gave an impatient sigh. 'OK, I guess I know. Only there must be other actresses with rich husbands. Hell, this is a great script and he's winning all the prizes these days. Why does he need her old man's money anyway? There must be plenty of backers.'

Jo surveyed the buttoned end of her foil. She said carefully, 'Perhaps it's the girl herself. She can be very charming.'

Carlos shot her a look of sheer incredulity. 'I've known Seb since we were at school. He doesn't let his affairs interfere with his work. And if he did——' He stopped at a distant call. 'That sounds like Lisa. I'll have to go get into my plumes,' he said. 'Let's continue this conversation later.'

But there was no further opportunity. The scene in the drawing-room had finished and Seb was at the bottom of the staircase already.

Jo could feel the impatience in him but he made sure everything was plotted and clear before he was satisfied. He took Carlos through his last moves while Jo went to be inserted into her wig.

Lisa was tumbling the red curls into artistic disorder when Simon came in. He looked harried. Jo thought that of all of them he would be getting the worst of Seb's drive to get the scenes finished.

He said rapidly, 'Change of plan. Seb wants you to go on fighting.'

Jo half turned. *'What?'*

Simon was impatient. 'Don't drop your foil on the fourth stair, as we rehearsed. Fight Carlos properly. Seb wants more spontaneity.'

Jo swung round on him and regarded him narrowly. 'Why?' she said at last.

Simon looked unhappy. 'He says it's because Carlos isn't a professional. The fights with the old guy are wonderful but he's being too careful with you. He doesn't know how to act. He's not spontaneous. So Seb says we've got to startle him.'

Jo said, 'That could be dangerous.'

Simon shook his head emphatically. 'The buttons on both foils are solid. I've checked them.'

Jo met his eyes and found that she believed him. 'What if he just stops the fight himself?' she objected dubiously. 'He might if he doesn't know what's going on.'

Again Simon shook his head. 'Seb told him not to. Carlos knows how important it is to keep on schedule.'

Jo said, 'Well, he's the director. It's up to him, I suppose.' But when Simon had gone she said drily to Lisa, 'Would you believe that man gave me a lecture this morning about not taking risks? *Me.'*

He had certainly done miracles in setting up the cameras in double-quick time, Jo thought with reluctant admiration. She skirted the cables carefully, making her way to the second floor by way of the back stairs. Across the landing of the first floor she saw Carlos in his feathered hat, and waved.

Just my luck if he drops his hat on me, she thought. She wouldn't blame him either. She did not approve of these on-film surprises, though she knew that other directors used them.

She took up her position inside the door that gave on to the second landing and waited for the signal. They were going to do the whole thing, trying to keep their faces out of camera focus. The stars would be filmed later in poses that arose spontaneously in the duel.

At the signal, she came out slowly as she and Carlos had rehearsed, looking behind her. He called out and she spun round as he ran up the staircase towards her, his foil pointing menacingly.

The next few moments went like clockwork. And though she felt him stiffen in surprise when she did not let him knock the foil out of her hand as they had rehearsed, he did not stop and demand an explanation. In fact, for a second she thought Seb must have been right because she could feel the strength Carlos had been holding back as he began to fight to disarm her in earnest. The camera would pick that up, Jo knew.

She could not last long against him, of course. She gave ground down the stairs. Her right arm ached and her wrist felt as if it were on fire. She could feel it weakening. And then as she feinted he lunged, hard and fast. She tried to parry but it was too late. The blade whipped across hers with a crack like breaking glass and her foil shot out of her hand.

Simultaneously Jo became aware of three things: her foil arcing through the air, a concerted shout from all around her, and a strange faintness. She watched the foil almost dreamily, faintly puzzled at its strange angle. Then she realised that her cheek was resting against a step and there was something warm trickling over her right hand. It was suddenly a great effort to turn her head.

When she did so, it was to find Seb's face on a level with her own. He looked murderous. Something else must be her fault. She felt her eyes fill with weak tears.

He said something. She couldn't make it out. For some reason her hearing was fuzzy. He was tearing at her coat and frilled shirt as if they were dish-rags.

Behind him Carlos was holding what seemed to be two knitting needles. He was looking sick. And Simon—Simon was backed up against the wall looking as if he had just found a corpse.

Suddenly Jo realised what had happened. She had let herself be tricked again. And this time she had got hurt. She laughed, and stopped as pain savaged the whole of the right side of her body.

Seb swore. This time she heard him.

'Don't move. You'll be all right, only don't move,' he said urgently.

His hands were still stripping the costume from her. He tipped her forwards so that her forehead was against his chest as he drew the jacket gently down her right arm. There was a gasp from the onlookers.

Jo looked down and saw that the sleeve of her muslin shirt had somehow turned red. Seb very gently turned her face away from the sight.

'You'll be all right,' he said again. 'Don't look.'

He was tying something very tightly round her arm. It hurt. She tried to say so but her tongue felt swollen. Her head swam.

Seb pulled her back against him, his hand cupping her face. It was crazy, she knew, but Jo felt deliciously protected. She gave a little sigh of surrender. For an instant she thought she felt his lips against her hair.

She did not, she felt muzzily, deserve this. She had made a terrible mistake. She had ruined the scene.

She mumbled, 'Anna Beth said I wasn't as clever as I thought I was. And I wasn't, was I?'

'Neither was I, my darling,' Seb said grimly.

She began to laugh but cut it off, wincing. Blackness began to creep round from behind her. She felt his arms tighten. It seemed as if she were flying. She felt a momentary alarm; then realised that he was still there, his chest rising and falling under her cheek. So she was not afraid any more; not as long as Seb was holding her.

Good grief, thought Jo, floating. I must be in love. She told him so, pleased.

He did not seem pleased. In fact he seemed ferociously angry, at least as far as she could tell. The darkness was opening and closing across her vision like camera shutters, faster and faster. She put up a hand to brush the camera shutters away and found it caught and held.

Seb's face, his eyes black with temper, swam before her. She wanted to explain, to apologise, to implore him not to be angry. But her head was lifting gently away from her body.

'Don't . . .' she began. But the words got away from her.

She did not even know that her head fell back against his shoulder as he lifted her into his arms and stood up.

CHAPTER NINE

SUN on her face and the scent of flowers: a delicious feeling of lassitude. She had come home at last. She could stop running.

Jo turned her head luxuriously against a cushion. It was scented with something herbal. She gave a little wriggle of well-being.

Someone said, 'You're awake, then.'

Her eyelids were heavy. She was reluctant to move. 'Grandpa?' she murmured.

'You've taken enough years off my life one way and another,' the voice agreed wryly. 'But no. Not your grandfather.' There was a creaking as if a chair had moved and then there were cool fingers on her face.

Reluctantly Jo came out of her stupor. Seb Corbel was looking down at her. She seemed to be in some sort of tent. The sun poured in over his shoulder. She squinted up at him, disorientated.

She was, she found, lying on a low divan. All around there was a blaze of geraniums. The heavy, honeyed scent of jasmine filled the air. And the sky was a blinding, shimmering blue. She struggled up on to one elbow among the cushions and immediately wished she hadn't.

'Where the hell am I?' she said, falling back with a wince.

Seb took his fingers away. 'Back fighting your corner by the look of it,' he said. He smiled down at her lazily. 'How are you feeling?'

Jo shook her head to clear it. She ran an exploratory hand over her right shoulder. 'As if I did three rounds with a combine harvester,' she offered.

He grinned. 'Not far off. Try an Olympic medallist.'

It came back then. With a rush. He had been furious and with reason. She fell back among the cushions, the back of her hand pressed to her eyes. 'Oh, my goodness.'

'Rather what I said,' Seb agreed amiably.

Jo took her hand away and looked at him cautiously. He didn't sound furious. 'What happened?'

He stretched lazily. Jo averted her eyes. She had a nasty suspicion that she had huddled into that khaki shirt as if it was her last hope of heaven.

'I was kind of hoping you'd tell me that.'

She explored her shoulder. It was solidly padded with linen bandaging but there was no disguising the dull throb that came from it.

'The button came off his foil?' she hazarded. 'I didn't really see. It all happened so fast.'

'Yes,' Seb said evenly. 'It did. The foil broke. Apparently it's been known to happen before, but very rarely. The jagged end went into your shoulder.'

'Oh,' said Jo. She thought about it. 'Does that mean another take?'

He looked momentarily startled. Then he gave a choke of laughter. 'Do you think you're up to it?'

Jo tried to rotate her shoulder and gave up. 'Not this afternoon.'

'Or for several days.' Seb paused. 'You lost quite a bit of blood.'

'Oh,' she said again.

For some reason she did not want to look at him. She made her fingers into a cat's cradle and studied them with concentration.

He said, 'Do you want something to drink? Pepita left some lemon. The doctor said you should rest and take lots of liquid.'

'Doctor?'

'The bandaging,' Seb said carefully, 'is a professional job. I only patched you up for the duration. We dug out a quack and he did the business and shot you full of pain-killers. Then I brought you here.'

Jo raised her eyes at that and, for the first time, registered the significance of the tubs of flowers and the sky above them.

'This is where Simon brought me first of all. The roof in Santa Ana.'

'And where he should have left you,' Seb said. 'None of this would have happened if you had been out of the house.'

'None of what?'

He stood up and went to the parapet, looking out over the roofs to the shimmering hillside. 'Why don't you tell me?' he suggested softly.

Jo did not know what to say.

'Starting,' prompted that inexorable voice, 'with why you decided to change the fight today.'

'But—that was you,' she blurted and then, remembering Simon's shocked face, stopped dead.

Seb turned neatly back to her. He leaned against the parapet, his hands in the pockets of his trousers, and smiled at her. He looked as if he had all the time and not a care in the world, Jo thought. Instead of which, he had a film to finish that was now seriously over schedule.

'No,' he said lazily. 'No, I liked the authorised version. With you disarmed on the fourth step. And so did Carlos, he tells me. So—what happened?'

'I thought... He said, spontaneity...' Jo said, not very lucidly.

Seb nodded. He did not look surprised; or even very interested. 'He?'

Jo met his eyes reluctantly. She said nothing.

'Jo, we've just had a serious accident. It could have been a lot worse. You must see that loyalty doesn't come into it. He's dangerous.'

She thought of Simon's tense unhappiness. 'No,' she said involuntarily.

Seb's face hardened, throwing the bones into harsh prominence. 'All right. I'll say it for you: Simon.'

Jo bent her head.

'And presumably he also told you to take that header off the cliff when you said you thought you were doing what I wanted,' he added, almost to himself.

She said swiftly, 'That wasn't dangerous. It just looked it. I knew what I was doing.'

'It was more dangerous than I asked for,' Seb said unanswerably. 'And that business with the horse was certainly dangerous. I've ridden that creature. She's not for the unwary.'

Jo gave him a level look. 'The horse was nothing to do with Simon.'

His mouth thinned. 'You're very loyal.'

She shook her head. It hurt her shoulder and she winced. 'No; I just don't like injustice. It isn't Simon who's been orchestrating accidents, and you know it.'

Their eyes met. Jo felt the clash of it jolt through her like a bolt of lightning.

Then he said, too evenly, 'There has only been one.'

She stared. 'Don't be ridiculous. What about my predecessor? And the girl before that? And the woman whose room I inherited? What happened to them? Spontaneous combustion?'

Seb's eyes were as light and cold as glass. 'You've been listening to gossip.'

Jo struggled upright. It made her head swim but she was so angry that she hardly noticed. 'So you're willing to hand the can to poor old Simon because he's junior and expendable and can't defend himself. While your girlfriend——'

'I think,' Seb said in his most indifferent voice, 'you'd better stop there. Before you say something actionable.'

Jo glared at him. 'I thought better of you. They all said that you were a bully who'd stop at nothing to get your movie shot but I'd come to believe they exaggerated. I see they didn't.'

His eyes narrowed. 'They? Who? More gossip? You seem to have a taste for it.'

Jo said furiously, 'I don't need to listen to gossip to see where your priorities lie: it shows. If you don't want it to, you shouldn't let her wrap herself round you at mealtimes.'

The moment she had said it she wished she hadn't. It sounded appallingly catty. It also sounded dangerously close to jealousy.

Seb took a step forwards; then stopped. He gave her a long, measuring look which she could not meet.

Then he drawled, 'You noticed. But why do *you* care, darling? Or is this high-mindedness for its own sake? I remember Jerry saying you didn't care for my lifestyle, whatever that means.'

Jo fought down her shame. 'You're right,' she said hastily. 'It's nothing to do with me——'

'I didn't say that,' he interrupted softly.

She raised her eyebrows. 'No? That's what it sounded like.'

'Then, as usual, you misunderstand me. I asked *why* it was your business.'

Jo was bewildered and it showed. Her shoulder was a dull ache and the blood was beginning to pound in her temples. She put a hand to her head. 'Don't play games with me,' she said in a voice that, no matter how hard she tried to steady it, she could not keep from breaking. 'I don't know what you want from me.'

Seb's face was unreadable. He stood like a statue. Then he said almost idly, 'Why don't you come out of that sanctuary of yours and find out?'

Her hand fell. She stared at him. Across the still terrace their eyes locked. There was not a sound. The heat beat up at Jo from the roof. The light was dazzling. She swallowed. It sounded like an avalanche in the taut silence.

He strolled over to her, his shadow very black and thin as a dagger. Jo shivered, but did not shrink away. His eyes noticed it, narrowing.

Seb said almost to himself, 'Not the best timing, Corbel. But not a lot of choice.'

He dropped on to one knee beside the divan and took her very gently by the shoulders. Jo caught her breath, waiting for the nightmare to strike.

But all she could feel was the warmth of his palms where they caressed her; the vibrancy of the rangy body that all her experience and the self-defence of a lifetime said was too close. Very slowly he leaned forwards and touched his mouth to her own.

Jo sat absolutely still. Seb's mouth moved, light as a cobweb, across her lips. There was no sense of suffocation, of dawning panic, just a slow, tingling pleasure. There was no fear in it.

Seb lifted his head. He gave a little sigh.

Then he pulled her hard against him and his mouth wasn't gentle any more.

Jo fell against him, her body pliant. His hands moved up and down her spine. She began to tremble. She touched his face, shyly, blindly. He made a small sound and his mouth left hers to travel down the offered arch of her throat. She was burning up. Her pulses were drumming. Her whole body was out of any control but his.

'Jo.' Against her skin his voice was muffled. 'My darling, gently.'

But the sensations were too new. She did not know what was happening to her. She reached for him, urgent hands sliding under the warm cotton of his shirt to the warmer skin beneath. Seb groaned.

And at that point there was a clattering on the stairs.

Seb jack-knifed away from her. He was on his feet in a second, running his fingers rapidly through his disarranged hair. Jo fell back, catching her breath as she jarred her injured shoulder.

From the steps Pepita appeared, bearing a tray. She was followed by Carlos Andrade looking worried.

There was a quick splutter of Spanish, then Pepita set down a tray by the divan and offered Jo a glass of cloudy liquid. Jo took it blankly, unable to tear her eyes away from Seb. He was frowning. She drank the stuff quickly and gave the glass back to Pepita, who went away.

Carlos said, 'How are you now?'

'I'm not sure,' Jo said slowly.

She thought she saw Seb wince. Carlos turned to him. 'Have you told her?'

Seb made a small movement as if he would hush Carlos but caught himself. 'No.' It was curt.

'For heaven's sake...' Carlos was impatient. 'They'll be here any minute.'

'They?' asked Jo.

Carlos hunkered down beside the divan. He looked very serious. 'The gentlemen of the Press, Jo. The hounds of the people. They've got wind of something. And Anna Beth's got her lawyers in. Even the Spanish police are beginning to get interested. Simon's had two calls apparently.'

'Simon?'

'They wanted to talk to me,' Seb said evenly. 'I didn't know. It seems to have slipped Simon's mind. So now they're suspicious—reasonably enough.'

In spite of the harsh sun, Jo began to feel cold. 'Suspicious about what?' she asked.

Seb lifted his shoulders. 'Too many accidents,' he said expressionlessly. 'As you said.'

'And—they'll want to see me?'

Seb did not answer.

After a quick, surprised look at him, Carlos said, 'The doctor reported your accident. I drove down to see the Captain of Police myself. That's when I heard about the news hounds. We'll have to be careful or there'll be a full-scale inquiry.'

'Ah,' said Jo. Seb took a half-step and stopped at the look on her face. She felt the ice settle round her as if she were packed in it. It almost hurt to make her jaw move. 'So Seb came to tell me to keep my mouth shut?'

It sounded rather good, she thought remotely. As if it didn't matter to her at all. Carlos, at any rate, noticed nothing wrong. He nodded emphatically.

'The girl's having hysterics. She's been on the phone to her husband about twenty times. And Simon Curtis looks as if he's having a breakdown. If we don't take the heat out of it—if the bloodhounds clap eyes on either of them—the scandal will be in the New York stop press today,' he said grimly.

Jo looked at Seb, who said, 'Since Simon's collapsed, Carlos has appointed himself his successor, you notice.'

'Well, someone has to,' Carlos returned. 'Do you want to get this damned film finished or not?'

Jo said softly, 'A conscientious director will do anything to finish his film, won't he, Seb?'

Preoccupied as he was, Carlos noticed that. He looked swiftly from one to the other, opened his mouth—and shut it again. Seb's expression was like granite.

She closed her eyes briefly. Whether it was Pepita's draught or the emotions of the last few minutes, her head was beginning to swim. Her shoulder began to thump with pain. She eased it against the cushions and opened her eyes.

'You needn't worry,' she told Carlos steadily. 'I shan't be accusing anyone of anything. I want this film finished as soon as anyone else. And,' the quiet voice was icy, 'a scandal won't do me any more good than it will Miss Arden.'

She did not look at Seb. There was an uncomfortable pause.

'That's sensible,' Carlos said at last, awkwardly.

Jo gave a little choke of laughter. 'I *am* sensible. Usually. Though when I make mistakes they're big ones.' There was no disguising the bitterness.

Seb said, half under his breath, 'Jo...'

But she raised her head and looked at him. 'How much longer will it take?'

Seb shook his head, shrugging. Carlos looked exasperated. Seb said almost absently, 'Depends on what today's stuff looks like. I'll work it out later. But anyway, you——'

Jo said, 'I'm patched up and the costume will hide the bandages. I'll be back to finish——' she hesitated '—what I contracted for.'

Seb said sharply. 'Don't be ridiculous.'

'It's not ridiculous.' Jo was very calm. She gave him a blinding smile that made her jaw ache. 'I can't afford people saying I don't give value for money. Not seeing how expensive I am,' she reminded him.

He acknowledged the hit, his jaw tightening. His eyes glinted with anger. But, being Seb, he did not explode. Jo wondered what it would take to make him lose that formidable control.

'Killing yourself is not the best way to do it, though,' he drawled.

She gave a brittle laugh. 'You're as dramatic as Miss Arden. A little work won't kill me. Don't forget, I'm tougher than I look.'

Seb looked at her for a long moment. 'Are you?' he said softly.

Jo looked away. 'Of course. It's my profession.'

Carlos broke in, 'Look, what are you going to *do*, Jo?'

She gave a long sigh. 'Whatever you want,' she said wearily.

Carlos gave a brisk nod. 'OK. The publicity girl's got a statement drafted. Do you feel up to talking in person?'

'No,' Seb said swiftly.

Jo ignored him. 'Of course.'

'Someone will bring you up to the house later——'

'I don't,' said Seb evenly, 'want her back in that house.'

Jo had thought that nothing could hurt her more than Seb had already, but she found she was wrong. She almost gasped at the pain of it.

Carlos was saying crisply, 'That's nonsense. Jo's right. You're as bad as the Arden girl. You're over-reacting.'

Seb said obstinately, 'No.'

He went on saying no. Jo found exhaustion getting the better of her. She drifted in and out of the conversation. Neither man seemed to notice.

In the end they settled that she would join the Press conference briefly, have supper with the others, talk to the police if they still wanted to see her, and come back to Pepita's to sleep. Pepita, when the plan was explained to her, was flatteringly delighted.

She fussed over Jo all afternoon. By the time the car came down from the house to pick her up, Jo was thoroughly rested and cared for. She was still shaky, though, when she went into the sitting-room to join the others.

A swift look round showed her Anna Beth, looking magnificent but unusually quiet, as well as Bill and Carlos. Seb was talking earnestly to a man she did not recognise. Of Simon there was no sign.

Chairs had been arranged in a semicircle round a sofa on which Anna Beth was already ensconced. The publicity assistant gave Jo a preoccupied smile and ushered her over to the sofa. Anna Beth stiffened.

Jo sat down with careful composure. She had seen the cameras. She gave Anna Beth a friendly smile. From the far corner of the room there was a flash. Anna Beth did not even jump. She had seen them too.

They were soon grouped artistically and the journalists took up their positions. Seb read a prepared statement. Then he answered questions easily, looking relaxed. Jo was impressed, though a master of deception would not find a Press conference particularly difficult, she thought, recalling that Seb, too, used to be an actor.

There were questions for Anna Beth, too, of course. Standing behind Jo, Carlos was tense as the actress answered. But Seb, to her right, stayed cool. For once Anna Beth was on her best behaviour.

Yes, the film had gone on longer than she had expected; yes, she very much enjoyed working with Sebastian Corbel; yes, she adored Spain.

They turned to Jo, balked. It was clear that they had got a hint of something, but not much of the truth.

Was it true that the stunts were so difficult that they had had to call her in as a troubleshooter at the last moment?

Jo said carefully, 'I wasn't going to do the film originally because it didn't fit with my schedule. After the delays, it did.'

'But your predecessor had trouble with things she was asked to do?' persisted a tall man with glasses and a French accent.

'I would very much doubt it,' Jo said smoothly.

'Then what's been happening?'

'You must bear in mind that stunting is a different business from acting. We're not usually needed for long. So we book ourselves more tightly. We haven't got the spare capacity to take too much overrunning on a schedule,' she said.

It sounded plausible. No one in the business would believe it, of course. One or two of the journalists looked sceptical, but it seemed to satisfy her enquirer.

To clinch it, she added, 'For example, I'm booked to go to Hungary in a week's time.'

And that was true. It had the unmistakable ring of truth, too. None of the journalists looked sceptical now.

Seb said pleasantly, 'So we have every reason for pressing on with filming as soon as Jo feels up to it. There are only a couple more scenes to do. Then we clear up the last of the principals' insets and we're off to the cutting-room.'

'And how long will that take?' one of the men asked.

Seb smiled. 'I see no reason to change the expected release date at this stage.'

There was a whistle of surprise from someone.

'Skimping on the cutting? That's not like you,' somebody said.

He laughed. 'Just a spot of late-night working.' He stood up with a glinting smile. 'See you at the première, ladies and gentlemen.'

There were photo-calls after that. Jo slipped away. Nobody was suspicious. They were all sympathetic about her accident.

She avoided the courtyard and the terrace where her former room had been. She was wandering into the library when Miguel found her.

'Good to see you in one piece,' he greeted her. 'That was a lot of blood you left behind. The girls have been scrubbing ever since.'

'Nonsense.' Jo smiled at him, although it was with an effort. She appreciated his attempt to lighten the atmosphere.

He shook his head. 'It was horrible. Nobody knew what to do. You should have seen yourself. You couldn't see your hand for blood. I thought Seb was going to kill someone.'

Jo bit her lip.

'She's been damned lucky,' Miguel said heavily.

Jo didn't pretend to misunderstand him. 'Let's hope it gives her a good fright.'

'She's had that, all right. After Seb talked to her, she looked as if he'd hit her.'

'I know the feeling,' Jo said drily. 'But he's still protecting her.'

Miguel said, 'He's hardly let her out of his sight since he found out you'd live. I think he's afraid to.'

Jo did not answer. So, she thought painfully, he must really love her. It was extraordinary how much that hurt.

And it was there for everyone to see that night at dinner and during the next day.

'Anna Beth's still stuck as close as sticking-plaster,' Lisa said, painting out the line of the wig, looking in the mirror at her handiwork. 'You'd think she'd be ashamed.'

'I guess she thinks she needs Seb,' Sue said, easing Jo's boots on and giving them a proprietorial buff. She looked up. 'He's been very—gentle with her.'

Lisa sniffed. 'Keeping her sweet till she's done her stuff.'

Jo said nothing. She did not have to. It was evident in every line of Anna Beth's subdued face that there was only Seb between her and purgatory. And Seb was treating her like precious china.

'Men,' said Lisa with loathing. 'Who needs them?'

'Yes,' agreed Jo on a little laugh that broke. And went out to do battle with him for the last time.

He was impeccably polite. He asked her how she felt. He took her through the ride, pacing beside her, a hand ready to take the horse's bridle. There were never less than three other people close to them at any one time. He never touched her or met her eyes. There was no lazy laughter in his voice, only crisp, impersonal instruction.

It was impossible to remember that he had ever touched her, still less kissed her until she was weak and willing in his arms.

They did it once. Perfectly.

'Run it through again,' Seb said pleasantly. 'We need all the insurance we can get.'

There was a ripple of laughter. Everyone went through the gallop and skid without complaining. When it was over, he thanked them all, his eyes skimming over Jo. Then he turned his back and went swiftly back to the Land Rover.

Jo watched him. As always, Anna Beth was with him. One long arm was round her waist. Her hair was tied back at the nape with a sliver of ribbon. In the mountain breeze, the curls blew on to Seb's khaki shirt like a badge of possession.

Jo remembered the shirt. Her mouth went dry, as she remembered slipping her hands under it, feeling Seb's blood beat against her palms and his breath quicken. And all to get her to do what he wanted. Just as Jerry had said.

She sat, dry-eyed, as Lisa removed the red curls for the last time. When she got back into her own light clothes, she gave a great sigh of relief.

'Thank goodness that's over,' Jo said with real feeling.

Sue nodded, smiling, but Lisa gave her an unexpectedly shrewd look. 'You'll get over it,' she said. 'They all do.'

Jo hung on to that thought all the rest of that day, saying her goodbyes. She did not see Seb—he was locked away, looking at the day's work—and she did not look too hard for Anna Beth. But she tracked down Simon Curtis.

'Will you take me to the airport?' she said.

Simon was looking wretched, almost ill. He stared. 'You *can't* want me to. You can't even want to see me,' he burst out.

Jo sat on the corner of his desk. 'Hey, you got conned. Don't take it to heart. It happens,' she said with irony, 'to all of us.'

'But I nearly got you killed,' he muttered.

Jo gave a snort. 'You got me a scratch and an injection and the best night's sleep I've had since I got here.'

He laughed involuntarily but said, 'Don't be nice to me, Jo. I don't think I can bear it.'

'OK,' she agreed. 'Drive me to the airport or I'll let your tyres down.'

'They're Seb's tyres,' he pointed out. But he looked happier. 'You win. I can't take another war with the great director.'

On the way they talked about the film and her next job and where Simon lived in England. Only once did he bring up the forbidden subject.

Pulling away from a petrol station, he said abruptly, 'You knew, didn't you?'

Jo looked carefully at the landscape which was speeding past them. Had she known about Seb and Anna Beth? It had seemed a possibility, certainly. But then there had been that gypsy, and it had not *felt* as if he was in love with her. It had not felt as if he was in love with anyone. Except that she was the last person in the world to know when someone was in love, she thought drearily. It had taken her long enough to work out that she was, herself.

'Not for sure,' she said at last.

Simon was not listening properly. 'And that was why you didn't want the job.'

She said coldly, 'The director's morals—and those of his cast—are nothing to do with me.'

Simon heard that, right enough. He took his eyes off the road to give her an incredulous look. Jo pointed this out to him and he looked obediently ahead again.

He said, 'I didn't mean her and Seb. I meant about what she was up to. With you and those others.'

'Oh. Her anti-rival campaign,' Jo said, enlightened. 'Let's just say I had worked with her before and I knew she was a little insecure.'

But he did not seize the offered excuse as he once would have done, and said soberly, 'She frightened herself this time, I think. She certainly frightened Seb.'

Jo drew a sharp breath. Of course, he would be frightened if he saw the woman he loved heading for the destruction of her career.

Simon said tentatively, 'I wouldn't have believed Seb could behave like that. He's always so cool, old Seb. As if there's nothing he can't handle.'

Jo shut her eyes. It didn't make it any more bearable but at least it kept back the tears.

Disappointed, Simon said no more. They talked pleasant nothings until he took her to the check-in desk. Then, hesitating a little, he bent forwards and gave her a clumsy kiss.

'See you at the première,' he said.

'Oh, no,' said Jo grimly. 'I'm out of that particular cage and you won't find me going back to the zoo. I've done it. It's over.'

And she turned and strode away, leaving Simon staring after her.

CHAPTER TEN

JO WORKED like a demon for two months. She got paler and thinner. Her grandfather was shaken out of his obsession with the threatened loss of his house when he saw her.

'What have you been doing to yourself?' he said involuntarily as Jo hoisted her overnight bag over her shoulder and got out of the car.

'Working,' Jo said briskly and not entirely truthfully.

Her grandfather came forwards with an anxious expression. 'Have you hurt yourself, then?' he asked, taking the bag from her.

Jo sniffed. 'I'm a professional,' she reminded him. 'I'm *paid* not to get hurt.'

He looked worried. 'Then you must be working too hard.' He accompanied her into the tiled entrance hall. He looked round at the gleaming floor, the sixteenth-century settle, polished so that it shone like velvet, the great seventeenth-century mirror over the hall fireplace. He swallowed.

'It's not because of the house, is it, Jo? I mean you're not beating the hell out of yourself because of your father and the mortgage?'

Jo was straightening her hair in the mirror and didn't answer immediately. Behind her she could see her grandfather's face creased in anxiety.

'It's only a house, Jo,' he said earnestly. 'It's not worth killing yourself for.'

Jo turned and gave him a swift hug. 'There's just a lot of work about at the moment. It's not the house. Or not specially.'

He looked relieved. But he stayed thoughtful. They went into the big flagged kitchen. He gave her a drink as she sat at the kitchen table and watched him put the finishing touches to their lunch. And they talked about Hungary and the new adventure film she had just been in, and the screening of an older film which he had seen on television in her absence abroad. Everything except Spain. It was not mentioned once. And, although he was always interested in her colleagues, he did not breathe a word about Anna Beth Arden, Bill Hamilton or Seb Corbel. It was almost as if he had been warned not to, Jo thought, suspicious but relieved.

And it wasn't until she was back in the car, ready to leave for London, that he said thoughtfully, 'I wonder what *is* worth it?'

Nonplussed, Jo stared. 'Worth what?'

'Killing yourself for,' her grandfather said tranquilly. 'Because that's what you're doing. You be careful, my girl. Or you're going to end up ill.'

Jo had no answer for that. So she gave him a fleeting, strained smile and drove away.

He was right of course. She knew it. So did all her friends. And even Jerry, who had a healthy interest in his percentage and was angelically discreet about her distress on her return from Spain, had remonstrated. But Jo was adamant.

'My father has gone quiet,' she said to Jerry in his London office. 'That means he's up to something. I've got a lawyer keeping an eye on things but he could still pull a surprise. He wants the Court. He could just turn up one day with a possession order or something. I can't pay off the mortgage yet but I'm jolly nearly there.'

'You're mad,' said Jerry, sighing. 'All right, go and do a couple of days scrambling in the Lakes for Perigord Television.' He looked at her narrowly. 'What about the new movie that Corbel is casting?'

Jo tensed, but she had had a lot of practice at not reacting to Seb's name by now.

So she said with every appearance of indifference, 'That's...what? Four months away? I hope I'll be able to take a holiday by then.'

'I'm glad,' Jerry said drily. She had the feeling he was not deceived. 'So I'll look for someone else, shall I?' Without waiting for an answer, he went on in a casual tone, 'Do you want an escort to the première, by the way?'

'Première?' Jo echoed, momentarily confused.

'*Dangerous Midnight*,' Jerry reminded her. 'Your invitation is here.'

'Oh, *no*,' said Jo in involuntary horror which she did not have time to disguise.

'Thought so,' said Jerry. He stopped being discreet and looked at her straight. 'You'll have to go, you know. Or there'll be talk.'

'I know,' Jo said miserably. 'After that silly girl laying about her like that. There's been talk already, hasn't there?'

Jerry shrugged. 'Nothing that need worry us. Nothing about,' he hesitated and then went on deliberately, 'about you and Seb.'

Jo flinched. She said nothing.

'I'm not asking what happened,' he said eventually. 'But you know the man's been bombarding the office with phone calls—wants your number, wants your address. Frankly, I don't know how he's got the time. He must be twelve hours a day in the cutting-room. But he clearly thinks you've got unfinished business.' He hesitated again. 'He's not going to give up.'

Jo said with difficulty, 'I didn't know.'

Jerry looked sober. 'I thought you had enough on your plate. And I thought if you'd had a row with him, he'd get over it. Only he hasn't. And I don't think it was a row.' It was a question.

'Well, only some of the time,' she admitted painfully.

'Poor old Jo.' He looked almost uncomfortable. 'I heard he was strong stuff but I thought you'd be able to look after yourself. You're not exactly susceptible. I pushed you a bit, too. I'm sorry, kid.'

Jo found she couldn't answer.

'You'll get over it,' he offered. 'We all do. And I'll ride shotgun at the première.'

He was as good as his word. It did not stop Jo getting ready for the formal opening with more trepidation than she had felt since she was a teenager going to her first party. But at least, she thought wryly, it meant that she did not have an accident in her car, driving herself into town.

Jerry turned up in a chauffeur-driven limousine bearing violets and an expression of determined good cheer. It got them through the cocktails and into their seats awaiting the obligatory royal presence. Seb, of course, was busy. Jo kept him in clear view and, whenever his head turned, withdrew strategically into the shadow of Jerry's shoulder.

The film was—rather to her surprise—very good. The stunts were, she thought critically, well placed to make an emotional impact. The dive into the lake had even that sophisticated audience gasping. Anna Beth, she thought drily, should go into directing. It had been her idea, after all.

Afterwards they had to remain in their seats while the royal party left. They were not part of the formal presentation, much to Jo's relief, but they would have to go to the big reception that followed. Jerry looked down at her.

'Half an hour. Just to be seen. Then you can go. You're working tomorrow,' he said encouragingly.

Jo was clutching his arm but she grinned weakly. She was making a commercial the following day. She had to dress up as a clown and climb a signpost. It would take a couple of hours at a scruffy West London studio and she did not have to be there until midday, as Jerry well knew.

'So I am. Stressful stuff. Early night essential.'

She went on saying that to everyone she met. After twenty minutes, while Jerry talked to the casting director of the new prestige British movie, Jo began to hope she could get away without the confrontation she feared. And then the back of her neck began to prickle with a familiar feeling.

She did not turn round. She did not need to.

'So there you are,' drawled Seb Corbel. 'I was looking for a wig and dark glasses.'

The very sound of his voice made Jo's heart contract in her breast. It's not *fair*, she thought furiously.

'Not up to facing me?' he mocked softly.

She did turn round then, keeping her face carefully expressionless. He was standing very close. In the formal dinner-jacket he looked bigger and somehow rather alarming. For no reason at all, the image of the gypsy flashed across Jo's memory, he would look like this in formal clothes: dangerous was the only word.

Jo gave Seb a smile. She concentrated on a point above his left ear. His fallen-angel look was pronounced and he looked as if he might set light to something at any moment. She refused to acknowledge it.

'How are you, Seb?'

'Exhausted, overworked, frustrated and in a flaming temper,' he told her pleasantly. 'And you?'

She ignored that too. It was safer. 'Oh—busy.'

'So I hear. Too busy to return my calls. Or so that damned agency tells me.'

Jo's smile began to hurt her lips. 'I've been away a lot,' she agreed.

'I'm not a fool,' Seb said crisply. 'You've been running away. You look like death on it. How are the nightmares?'

Jo almost jumped. In the strain and the all-too-often sleepless nights of the last weeks, she had forgotten the crippling nightmare.

Seb read her expression. 'Gone, are they? Got some new ones?'

Jo said stiffly, 'I don't know what you mean.'

The long, beautiful hands moved. Jo thought he was going to touch her, and tensed. But the gesture was curbed almost before it began. Seb smiled like a tiger. He was very angry.

'Oh, yes, you do. Even if you've been editing your memory, your body remembers.'

Jo looked round wildly. There was no one in the immediate vicinity but there easily could have been. He was making no attempt to keep his voice down.

'For heaven's sake,' she muttered.

'Doesn't it?' The brown eyes bored into her. 'Mine does,' he told her almost conversationally. 'I haven't got you out of my mind for a single hour since. I feel as bad as you look. How long are you going to keep us both on the rack, Jo?'

Her pulses leapt in uncontrollable response. She said in a panicky under-voice, 'You're crazy.'

'Probably.' Suddenly Seb had relaxed. He sounded almost amused. 'Whose fault is that? Let's find somewhere quiet and discuss it.'

'No.' It was almost a scream. Heads turned. Jo felt her skin flood with colour. It did not dispose her any the more kindly towards the tormentor now laughing at her over his champagne glass. 'I wouldn't go on a last lifeboat with you. I don't trust you,' she hissed. 'We have nothing to say to each other.'

Seb was unmoved. He continued to look at her in that unnerving, assessing way. 'You could be right,' he mused.

Jo looked round. Jerry had not seen her plight. He was still absorbed in what was clearly business. She began to gabble.

'I need to get home. Early start. Rather tired...'

'I'll take you,' Seb said calmly.

She looked at him, appalled. 'But you can't. It's—I mean the party—the guests—what will people *say*?'

His smile was wry. 'They will say what they've been saying for months. That I can't keep my eyes off you. Or my hands. And that I'd better do something about it before I kill someone.'

'Oh.' She was utterly silenced.

He took a step towards her. He did not touch her but she could feel the heat of him against the bare skin of her shoulders. And, the way he was looking at her, touch was irrelevant. She shivered.

'Jo, I know you were angry,' he said in a low voice. 'You had every reason to be. And scared. You had reasons enough for that too, heaven forgive me. Only...'

She could not bear the way he was looking at her. She might just as well have been in his arms. And people were beginning to eye them covertly. Seb seemed unaware of it.

Jo gritted her teeth and said in a level voice, 'I'm tired. I've got a full schedule. I'm going home.'

She was already turning away as he said, 'Bolting back to prison? It doesn't make a lot of sense, you know, Jo.'

The husky voice reacted on her nerves like a caress. She thought, I can't let him do this to me. I *won't*. She didn't answer or look back.

As she strode through the room, Seb stayed at her shoulder. She was almost certain that he was laughing. He said her name, on that powerfully seductive note, once. But he seemed more amused than anything else when she did not even turn her head. By the time she reached the door she was shaking as much with temper as the force of her reluctant attraction to him.

'You're a stubborn woman,' he said, falling back. He did not sound disappointed, she thought savagely. Or as if he cared very much at all. Presumably it had been worth a try to see if he could seduce the unseduceable but, when he lost the game, he was not bothered.

Well, she was very glad to know. It was no more than she had suspected—except that she would never have expected him to make another attempt on her defences. She did not quite see why he had—except that he clearly regarded it as a very good game.

Jo left a message for Jerry with one of the waiters and asked the doorman to call her a cab. In a high old fury at being a source of amusement for Seb Corbel, she got herself home.

Once in the small flat, however, reaction set in. It was not new. It had happened the first day she got back from Spain. And every day since when she had not been so tired that she had fallen straight into bed. Not for the first time, Jo wished that she had never taken the job, never met Seb Corbel, never had the heart torn out of her by a lazy sophistication she could not begin to match. She buried her head in her hands, too despairing for tears.

When the doorbell rang, she picked up the entry-phone without much interest. It was probably her next-door neighbour forgetting his key again.

The voice at the front door was more than usually incoherent. Francis must be celebrating, Jo thought, remembering the party she had just come from. Tonight everyone in the world was celebrating except herself. She pressed the release button to let him in.

Music, she thought. That's what I need. Something nice and orderly and philosophical.

She found something, put it on the stereo and huddled into the corner of the ancient sofa while soothing strains of Handel poured, unheeded, over her.

She had thought she was safe. She had thought that, because of what her stepfather had done, because of the rejection of her parents, she was never going to be vulnerable to another human being ever again; still less hunger like this over a man she knew was unavailable.

How could she have been so stupid? Within hours of meeting Seb she had been seeing everything in a different light—herself; her job; the nameless gypsy with his predator's prowl. That night at the fiesta she had virtually thrown herself at the gypsy. She had never done anything like it in her life. Never, before she met Seb.

Jo pushed fingers that trembled through her silky hair. She had to get this back into perspective.

'I wonder if it's irreversible?' she said out loud.

There was a loud knocking at the door. She jumped. Then she shrugged. It wouldn't be the first time that Francis had forgotten his key after an evening congratulating his staff on a new deal. Jo had a spare. She fished it out of the bureau drawer and went to the door.

The moment she began to open it, the door was pushed violently. Jo jumped back. And Seb Corbel walked into the room grinning.

'You should never open the door without knowing who's outside,' he said outrageously.

Jo gaped at him. He closed the door with exaggerated gentleness and propped himself up against it, surveying her. The gentle music flowed round them. The air in the flat seemed suddenly very hot and still.

Seb was no longer immaculate. Somewhere in the intervening period he had discarded his bow-tie, and his jacket now hung negligently over his shoulder, suspended from one finger. His hair was rumpled, curling on to his collar and pushed back from his brow as if he had been running his fingers through it. He looked lithe and vital and ready to pounce.

He looked like the gypsy.

Jo put a hand to her throat. 'Who——?' she began. But she was not allowed to finish. Seb stopped her by the simple expedient of reaching out and laying his thumb across her parted lips. Jo's whole body clenched. Every single word she had ever known fled straight out of her head.

'Nobody gave you away. You've got good friends, I'll say that for you. I followed your taxi. I've always wanted to do that, and this evening I made it. Jumped a red light or two, but what the hell?' It was said lightly, laughingly, but his eyes were not laughing. His eyes were passionate.

Jo said in a voice that did not sound like her own, 'What are you doing here?'

He gave that lop-sided grin that turned her bones to water and cradled her face between his hands.

'Well,' he drawled, 'you said you didn't want to talk. So I'll have to be inventive.'

He bent and kissed her with a slow, savouring thoroughness that made her want to weep. Oh, *why* did it have to be this laughing playboy? If it had to be anyone at all, why Seb Corbel?

'Any suggestions?' he murmured, laughing against her mouth.

Jo closed her eyes and said, 'Seb. I know you think I'm tough as old boots. But I'm not. Please don't do this to me. Don't you see, I can't *afford* it?'

He did not pretend to misunderstand. 'Jo, my love, I haven't got any choice.' He held her away from him and looked down into her eyes. What she saw in his face stopped her breath in her throat. 'And nor, I think, have you,' he said very gently.

Jo gave a little sob. She was ashamed of herself the moment it was uttered. Seb's arms tightened fiercely.

'Darling, listen to me. No——' as she moved '——no, just listen, for once. I know the film was a bad experience for you in lots of ways, some of them my fault. I'll make it up to you, I promise. But this—this is too important to throw away. You might not want to admit it to me. But you know, don't you? That night at the fiesta. If Simon and Anna Beth hadn't come along, we'd have stayed together then. We both knew it.'

He didn't just look like the gypsy; he *was* the gypsy. That must have been why the gypsy always looked so familiar. Why had she not recognised him before? Or had she not allowed herself to recognise him? Had she realised, deep in her subconscious, that the attraction was blood- and bone-deep and way beyond resisting from the first moment? So that if she was to defend herself at all during working hours, she had to split off the all-powerful director from the imagined lover?

Jo said slowly, 'I've been very stupid.'

Seb was holding her against him. His heart was racing but he was holding her lightly, rubbing his face over and over her hair.

'Not alone. And not unassisted. When I realised what that delinquent female was up to, I could have done murder,' Seb said. 'Can you ever forgive me?'

'Delinquent female?' Jo echoed. 'But—do you mean Anna Beth Arden?'

His lips moved against her temple. 'Mmm? Oh, of course I do,' he said absently.

Jo pulled away from him. 'Seb Corbel, if you go all absent-minded director on me now, I swear I'll strangle you,' she said, bounced out of her panic by sheer surprise. 'I thought you were in love with the girl.'

'*What?*' There was no mistaking the blank astonishment. He stared down at her. 'Why on earth...? Even before you arrived, she was nothing but the most confounded nuisance. Everyone knew it. *How* could you think...?' He stopped, and a look of disgust crossed his face. 'No. Don't tell me. Let me guess. My so-called reputation. Jerry told me about that right from the start. How could you be so stupid? A couple of sub-literate articles in the fanzines and you had me down as the twentieth-century answer to Don Giovanni.'

Jo removed herself from his arms. 'I don't read sub-literate articles,' she said with great dignity. 'People *told* me. All your female subordinates fell in love with you. And you liked it.'

A faint flush appeared over the prominent bones. Seb looked briefly discomposed.

'Well, once, maybe. My first film. I was very young and very pleased with myself. But that was fifteen years ago, for heaven's sake. And it's against all my principles to have sexual relationships with colleagues. Why do you think I was so angry when I found myself falling for you? It was downright *amateur*.'

Jo said neutrally, 'I thought you were angry with me.'

He groaned. 'Well, of course I was. Making me feel like that. Against all my principles. Messing up a film that was already a bitch. When I needed all my concentration on the work in hand. Do you know that I used to go over the next day's scenes and half the time I was fighting off the urge to come along the gallery to your room?'

'Oh,' said Jo again. She swallowed. 'No. I didn't know.'

'Well, thank goodness for that, at least. I was afraid I was totally transparent. Carlos saw it. And that damned girl wanted all my attention.'

'And got it,' Jo said waspishly. As soon as it was out she wished it unsaid. It sounded horribly close to jealousy.

Seb looked down at her, interested. 'Ah. So that's what you thought,' he said with a certain satisfaction. 'Look at it from my point of view. She is attractive, mildly talented and has had mountains of publicity in the States. She didn't seem a bad choice, given that I didn't want an out-and-out star. Mind you, if I'd known her husband had taken a stake in the thing, I wouldn't have cast her. It's just placing weapons in the backers' hands. But by the time I found out it was too late. And by the time you arrived it was damn nearly all shot. I couldn't afford a fight with her.'

Jo said, 'She seemed to have a hold over you. I thought it was love.'

'That,' said Seb smugly, 'shows how little you know about love. As I suspected. Come here.'

She evaded him. 'That first night,' she said with a little difficulty. 'You'd been out with Anna Beth. I saw you bring her back. She was practically dancing. I thought—that is, I didn't recognise you. I thought you were a gypsy.'

'I took her to see some flamenco,' he said impatiently. 'She wasn't getting the feeling for the dancing at all ...' He stopped then. His eyes lit with humour. 'Didn't recognise me? So what happened at the fiesta? Are you telling me you didn't recognise me then?'

Jo went scarlet. She felt she could very easily hate him.

She said between her teeth, 'It's not surprising. Or,' she added with a flash of vitriol, '*funny*. You didn't look like that during the day. Or behave like that. It was dark...'

But Seb was laughing helplessly. 'So what did you think you were doing at the fiesta? We damned nearly made love under the trees up there. Are you saying you thought I was a *stranger*? And you've got the gall to complain about my reputation.'

'I didn't... I wasn't thinking... It got out of control...'

'It did that, all right,' said Seb, grinning.

'Stop laughing at me, damn you. I had a dreadful time thinking I'd turned promiscuous,' Jo hissed. 'I knew it was your fault, of course...'

'Interesting,' said Seb. He reached for her and took her against his body again. Although he was still chuckling it was very clear that he had no intention of letting her go. 'You didn't recognise me but it was my fault. It sounds just like every marriage I've ever heard of. When's the wedding?'

She pushed against his chest. 'I didn't *have* to recognise you. Not that night. You were getting at me all day and every day. Touching me, making me think about my feelings. And that night you heard me making a noise and came to my room—do you remember? I'd never told *anyone* about the nightmare before. I suddenly felt so—vulnerable.'

He was not laughing any more. 'Yes. That was rather a revelation. For both of us, I'd say. That was when I realised how serious it was. For me.' He lifted one hand and very gently stroked her hair back from her face. The hand, Jo realised, astonished, was trembling. 'I want you, Jo. I need you, I think. I certainly need to be with you. I've never... There have been ladies, I don't deny it. It was fun and it was mutual; nobody got hurt. You could hurt me. Badly, I'm afraid.'

It was so unexpected that she had nothing to say. She searched his face: the deep-set eyes were no longer lazy or cynical but desperately sincere. Seb Corbel losing his cool at last, she thought. She gave a little sigh. Without fuss she reached up and kissed him.

For several whirling seconds she clung to him, her heart beating madly. When at last they broke apart, they were both gasping.

'Right,' he said almost grimly. 'That's it. When's the wedding? No later than three weeks. After that I'm in LA.'

Jo lay against him, trying to bring her tortured lungs under some sort of control. As his words sank in she raised her head. 'Wedding?' she said uncertainly.

His eyes gleamed. 'I'm too old for your Bohemian ways,' he said virtuously. 'I want marriage and commitment. No more mucking about with anonymous gypsies in Mediterranean woods for you. It's about time you settled down. I could,' he added, clearly pleased with the idea, 'probably reform you.' He swung her off her feet in a neat movement that Jo, the professional, did not see coming. 'Bedroom this way?' he asked in parenthesis. 'Thought so. Yes, it is my clear duty to save you from yourself.'

He dropped her gently on the bed and struck a noble attitude. Jo tried not to laugh, and failed.

'At great self-sacrifice, no doubt,' she teased.

'Absolutely.' He was unbuttoning his shirt. His eyes laughed at her but they were warm with passion. For the first time in her life Jo felt wholly confident and at peace. She reached forwards and brushed his hands away, unbuttoning the shirt herself. She slid it off him, shivering with delight at the feel of his skin under her hands. He bent and kissed her shoulder where the copper dress bared it. As he raised his head she turned her mouth, and on the long, soft kiss they fell together into a web of delight that Jo had never begun to imagine.

A century later she lay sleepily against his shoulder. He had one arm round her while, with the other hand, he brushed the soft hair away from her face. She sensed him watching her and smiled at him, though her own eyes were closing. She felt warm and loved and deliciously confident.

'You make me feel wonderful,' she said drowsily.

'Reform not going to be too much of a hardship, then?' he teased.

Jo lifted a hand and touched his cheek. 'Easy peasy.' A thought crossed her mind, faintly disturbing. She struggled back from the shores of sleep. 'Seb—you said—you didn't really think I was mercenary, did you? You kept going on about how much you were paying me——'

'That was me trying to remind myself you were on the payroll and off limits,' he said drily. 'Forget it. And Jerry told me about your grandfather's house. That's a fair old clutch of awful relatives you've got there, Miss Page. Fortunately I am not only sufficiently well off to clear that mortgage before you snap in two doing it yourself, I have a first-class family you will like.'

Jo closed her eyes and grinned. 'Irresistible,' she said, slurring it only a little.

Seb kissed her hair. 'You'd better believe it.'

Jo was almost asleep. 'I wish...'

He settled her more comfortably against him. 'Yes, my darling? What do you wish? A trip to the moon? A castle at the bottom of the sea? A magic guitar?'

Jo gave a long sigh. She kissed his shoulder. 'No, I just wish... I mean, that night at the fiesta. I was *shameless*. I just wish,' she continued on a rush, 'that I hadn't done it *first*. I mean, you were always so in control. It would have been nice,' she said wistfully, 'if you'd lost your cool before. If you see what I mean.'

Under her cheek his chest was shaking with laughter.

'Not very liberated, are you?' he taunted.

Jo shut her eyes tight. 'I'm not debating women's rights with you when I've just been to bed with a man for the first time,' she said with dignity.

He kissed her swiftly. '*Me* for the first time. Forget the rest,' he told her. 'And actually,' a note of unholy mischief came into his voice, 'I'm afraid I may have misled you a little.'

Jo was sufficiently surprised to open her eyes.

He was leaning over her, the brown eyes gleaming, as if they had never known how to look like ice. He kissed her again. 'I didn't correct you at the time. But I didn't *exactly* come into your room that night because you were having a nightmare. It was actually a fairly quiet nightmare.'

Jo's eyes grew round. 'You mean...'

'Uh-huh. I lost the battle.' Seb was not noticeably repentant. 'Seems to have become a habit. We'd better get married soon.'

Jo wrinkled her nose at him. 'Who are we reforming here? Me or you?'

'Both,' he said promptly. 'Will you? When?'

Jo shut her eyes again. Somnolence curled round her irresistibly. 'Yes,' she said, keeping it short in order to reply before she finally dissolved into sleep. 'Whenever you say.'

She felt herself turned slightly and gathered against his warm strength. She remembered with vast surprise that she had once been afraid of this.

'Thank goodness for that,' Seb said softly in her ear. 'At least you stop fighting the director when it matters.'

But Jo was asleep.

Following the success of WITH THIS RING,
Harlequin cordially invites you to enjoy the
romance of the wedding season with

TO HAVE AND TO HOLD

BARBARA BRETTON
RITA CLAY ESTRADA
SANDRA JAMES
DEBBIE MACOMBER

A collection of romantic stories that celebrate the joy,
excitement, and mishaps of planning that special day
by these four award-winning Harlequin authors.

**Available in April at your favorite Harlequin
retail outlets.**